A SUPERB NEW NOVEL FROM AMERICA'S AGATHA CHRISTIE

"An especially intricate puzzle, done in the best of her agreeably urbane manner."

—*The New Yorker*

"Emma Lathen—what more need one say to assure a best of the year in detecting?"

—*Newsweek*

"I keep saying 'urbane, witty, faultless, delightful'; what other adjectives is one to use for Lathen's precise blends of formal detection and acute social satire?"

—Anthony Boucher,
The New York Times Book Review

"Some authors are competent. Some few hit the heights. And on the height of heights is Emma Lathen. . . . She is peerless in style, wit, inventively credible plotting and character bits."

—Dorothy B. Hughes,
Los Angeles Times

SWEET AND LOW
was originally published by Simon and Schuster.

Books by Emma Lathen

Accounting for Murder*
Ashes to Ashes*
Banking on Death
Come to Dust
Death Shall Overcome
The Longer the Thread*
Murder Against the Grain*
Murder Makes the Wheels Go 'Round
Murder to Go*
Pick Up Sticks*
A Place for Murder*
A Stitch in Time
Sweet and Low*

* Published by POCKET BOOKS

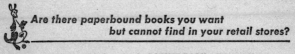

SWEET
AND LOW

EMMA LATHEN

PUBLISHED BY POCKET BOOKS NEW YORK

SWEET AND LOW

Simon and Schuster edition published 1974

POCKET BOOK edition published July, 1975

This is a work of fiction. The characters, names,
incidents, places and dialogue are products of the
author's imagination, and are not to be construed
as real.

⌐**L**

Standard Book Number: 671-78968-6.
Library of Congress Catalog Card Number: 74-2344.
This POCKET BOOK edition is published by arrangement
with Simon & Schuster, Inc. Copyright, ©, 1974, by Emma
Lathen. All rights reserved. This book, or portions thereof,
may not be reproduced by any means without permission
of the original publisher: Simon & Schuster, Inc., 630 Fifth
Avenue, New York, N.Y. 10020.
Front cover photograph by Fred Samperi.
Printed in the U.S.A.

SWEET
AND LOW

1

Men, as well as money, make Wall Street the entrepôt of the whole civilized world. Despite the claims of both friend and foe, these indigenes are not a breed apart. Qualifying as an actuary does not exempt anyone from the human condition. Hedge-fund operators are mortal; letter-stock specialists have been known to bleed.

True, even the mightiest of them is dwarfed by his awesome surroundings. Of course, so are the inhabitants of Grindelwald, Denver, and Lima. But mountains have a better reputation than other high rises. Say Everest or Jungfrau, and you conjure up men to match them; say World Trade Center, and you evoke automatons mistaking profit for enrichment.

Nothing could be further from the truth. Passions unconnected with negotiated commissions reverberate up and down Wall Street, as John Putnam Thatcher could attest. Certainly, his own particular monadnock, the Sloan Guaranty Trust, would function more efficiently if its personnel were immune from the frailties of the flesh. But as senior vice-president of the third largest bank in the world, Thatcher had file cabinets bulging with evidence of an incontrovertible truth. Initialing contracts, programming computers, and underwriting pilot programs are occasionally arduous, often inconvenient, and always insufficient to extirpate the Old Ned lurking below.

In fact, Thatcher had long since decided that Wall Street saw more of the real man than most other locales. With all deference to Sigmund Freud and the animal appetites, Wall Street—and the world it serves—proves

7

that sex is not the only outlet for deep-rooted, life-shaping forces. There are also buying and selling.

Zero population growth was going to get here a lot sooner than the day the New York Stock Exchange had to close its doors.

It was Thatcher's taxi mate, Bartlett Sims, who had prompted these musings. Sims, an octogenarian, had necessarily retired from a good many frays, but not from Waymark-Sims. Come hell, high water, or six inches of snow, Sims hauled himself into the office from Amagansett three days each week. Thatcher did not attribute this tenacity solely to the chauffeured Silver Cloud. Plenty of senior citizens were taking the IRT to get the best tonic in the world, an opportunity to watch the younger generation—Hugh Waymark was in his midfifties—mismanage everything.

The points he scored added years to Sims' life expectancy and, judging from the sound of it, there was a good chance he would live to be a hundred.

"Three or four years ago," Sims was saying, mellow with self-congratulation, "I said to Hugh, Hugh, now's the time for us to move into the Japanese market. Why leave all the gravy to Burnham? Hugh, I said, you've got to keep yourself flexible. No use getting stuck in a rut."

"Did you?" said Thatcher appreciatively.

"Well," said Sims, puffing out mottled cheeks, "you know the rest!"

Thatcher did indeed. The Japanese stock market was the last-but-one in a long line of Wall Street Loreleis. Like Xerox, conglomerates, and convertible debentures, it had been the legendary pot of gold at the end of some local rainbows. Those happy few blessed with foresight got more than sordid, material gain. They got brief immortality. Going into Japan at the right time was like predicting exactly when Dow-Jones would reach five—or fifteen—hundred. Those less fortunate admired and lamented. Very few lost loves cast an enchantment as enduring as Polaroid.

Like most winners, Sims was not unduly modest about

his coup, but it did not lead him to forget that these days he was conserving his strength.

"That's what they all keep after me about," he said, scornfully lumping together family, associates and medical advisers. "So, I had to give up sitting on the Leonard Dreyer Trust."

Thatcher recognized this pruning for what it was. Service to the community and other worthy pursuits were invariably the first to go. "Your term was up, too," he pointed out.

Sims accepted the technicality in good part. "Fought tooth and nail, but I got them to build the Dreyer Medical Center," he reminisced. "Up until then it was all the Dreyer Museum. Or the Dreyer Arboretum. Or the Dreyer Bach Choir, for Christ's sake. I just hope"—here he bent a bleak eye on Thatcher—"that you can do as well."

Thatcher had known Sims too long to be offended, which was fortunate since the old tartar continued: "I'm glad they named you the new trustee, John. I suppose you couldn't get out of it, no matter how hard you tried?"

"I'm going up to Dreyer tonight, for my first trustees' meeting," said Thatcher repressively. He had not sought out old Sims for a review of the convulsions which had culminated in his appointment as the newest member of the Leonard Dreyer Trust. He had already given the Sloan's president and the chairman of the board the benefit of his thinking on that subject.

"Not a bad bunch, on the whole," said Sims.

Considering the source, this was an accolade to the twenty-three distinguished citizens whose responsibility it was to oversee allocation of the large sums available to the Leonard Dreyer Trust.

"Of course, there are those college presidents and ministers," Sims said roundly. "Be sure to keep an eye on them. They've always got a million good ways to spend money. I've argued myself hoarse trying to explain that you can't spend what you don't have." Exasperation darkened his brow. "Honest to God, sometimes they're as bad as the United Way!"

Generosity wars with prudence in every charitable organization. But Thatcher's current interest was how the sides at the Leonard Dreyer Trust lined up. So he sidestepped the United Way and proceeded:

"With Howard Vandevanter on the trust ex officio, you didn't have to fight the battle of the balance sheets by yourself, Bart. If he can't tell the trustees the facts of life, nobody can."

Even Sims could scarcely claim to be the solitary champion of budgetary restraint at the Leonard Dreyer Trust, but his agreement was ungenerous. "Vandevanter couldn't fight his way out of a paper bag," he snorted.

Since Thatcher had heard him say the same of Hugh Waymark and Bartlett Sims, Jr., he was not overly impressed. Whether Howard Vandevanter relished infighting or not, he had to pack a punch at the Leonard Dreyer Trust, because he was president of the Dreyer Chocolate Company. And Leonard Dreyer's munificent bequest consisted of one million, three hundred thousand shares of common stock and forty-four thousand shares of preferred stock of the Dreyer Chocolate Company. The trust's income came from profits made on the sale of the most famous chocolate bar in the world.

Belatedly, Sims recalled that he was now above the battle. "Still, Vandevanter does the best he can. Then there's Yeoman. He's got a pretty good head on his shoulders—for a politician."

Thatcher recalled some of the literature that had already reached his desk. "When you're a Philadelphia Yeoman and you've served one term as governor of Pennsylvania, I believe you're called a public servant."

"Whatever you call him," Sims ignored distinctions, "Yeoman's nobody's fool."

But even this tempered praise went against the grain, so he added: "Although I always said that he isn't the best man to represent the trust on the company's board of directors. What you want there is a financial man. And

Yeoman doesn't know as much as he thinks he does. Pressuring Dreyer to raise dividends is all very well sometimes, but not when cocoa prices are skyrocketing. But try telling Yeoman that!"

He was rudely interrupted. The taxi had stopped for a red light. Suddenly, above the prevailing din, there was an ominous squeal, metal crunched against metal, and a rocking thump jolted the cab forward, scattering pedestrians like pigeons.

Thatcher and Sims were still disentangling themselves when the cabby pushed himself off the steering wheel. "Jesus! You people okay?"

Before Thatcher could report that all was well in the back seat, the driver had flung himself out of the cab. Sims, meanwhile, angrily retrieved the homburg that had been knocked to the floor.

"I can't see what hit us," Thatcher said after craning to look out the rear window. A solid wall of humanity blanketed them.

Bartlett Sims did not care. "We're only a few blocks from my office—and the walk will do me good! Call me anytime you want to talk—"

With that he liberated himself, disappearing immediately into the crowd.

Resolutely, Thatcher set aside a temptation to do likewise. He had work demanding his attention at the Sloan and a solemn promise to his secretary to make this a Thursday to remember. Furthermore, those letters and Miss Corsa were even closer to hand than Waymark-Sims.

But, like Hugh Waymark, for whom he spared a flicker of sympathy, he was not as freewheeling as old Sims. He was not ready to abandon Checker Cab driver Joseph Jerszy (No. 948576k) to his fate. There was also the small matter of the fare. Opening the door, Thatcher plunged toward the second car, which was fifteen feet behind its victim, canted to the curb. In front of the crushed radiator, their feet solidly planted in a widening

11

pool of oily green antifreeze, both drivers were bellowing at each other across a large, phlegmatic policeman.

". . . just rented the car this morning." The culprit brandished a sheaf of documents. "I'm a stranger here myself. In Akron . . ."

"Strangers shouldn't drive in New York!" Thatcher's cabby retorted. "How come you got to rent a car? We got subways! We got buses! We got taxis . . . !"

"What am I supposed to do now? Will the Avis people send me another car?"

Throughout these simultaneous monologues, the policeman wrote steadily, including Thatcher in his bill of particulars. In time, a tow truck arrived and this vignette of city life dissolved. When last seen, the gentleman from Akron was looking around as if expecting the heavens to open and deliver a four-door sedan with full options.

Why, Thatcher wondered, did his compatriots regard the automobile as an inalienable right, not a consumer durable? These caustic thoughts carried him to within a block of the Sloan where he was hailed.

"John, did you catch the docking?"

Thatcher greeted Charlie Trinkam, his second-in-command at the trust department. Incorrigibly insouciant, Charlie was the only member of the Sloan who could saunter down Exchange Place.

"Oh, did they finally find each other?" asked Thatcher, without slackening his brisker pace. "I've been having lunch with Bartlett Sims. We didn't see the news."

Charlie had the gift of pithy communication. "Yes. It was beginning to look as if NASA and the Russians would never get those space labs together. They've been missing connections up there for two days now. You know, for a bunch of high-powered types they seem pretty butter-fingered to me. They're always forgetting to tighten a screw or something."

Thanks to his recent experience, Thatcher was inclined to be more charitable. "At least they didn't run into each other."

"Wait until they get more traffic up there," Charlie said darkly. "They'll turn it into the New Jersey Turnpike."

"Or lower Broadway," said Thatcher, going on to describe his own vehicular adventure.

Charlie could take space exploration or leave it. "How was old Bart?" he asked.

"The same as ever," Thatcher replied.

Charlie's interest in Sims too was minimal but, like everybody at the Sloan, he liked to keep up with Thatcher's doings.

Another valued subordinate was bolder. "I hope you and Sims had a fruitful discussion about the Dreyer Trust," said Everett Gabler, when they encountered him at the elevator. Unlike Charlie, Everett was the embodiment of public and private virtue.

"That's right," said Charlie, snapping his fingers. "You're the new trustee, aren't you, John? Well, better you than me."

At no time did Everett approve of Charlie. When it came to such solid and substantial philanthropies as the Leonard Dreyer Trust, they were miles apart. But, being no fool, he did not try to melt stone with a recital of good works. Instead, he said: "I understand the trust distributes between eight and ten million dollars every year. I'm sure you'll agree that John's advice will be a significant contribution—"

Innate perversity led Charlie to remonstrate. "Oh sure, sure," he said, infuriatingly. "But don't claim dealing with the Dreyer Chocolate Company is going to be anything but a pain in the neck. I like conservative management as well as the next guy—but they're carrying things too far. Somebody should tell them that World War II is over."

Fortunately, Billings, the elevator operator, had delivered them to the sixth floor so Thatcher was able to escape. Irreconcilable disagreements between Charlie and Everett were neither new nor alarming. But before Thatcher emplaned for Dreyer this afternoon, he had better ways of spending his time, such as placating Miss Corsa.

13

Could he legitimately plead a traffic accident?

Before he had completely made up his mind, he was in Miss Corsa's office.

"Mr. Vandevanter called," she reported composedly. "Dreyer will have a car waiting for you at the Albany airport. You have a reservation at the Royal Dutch Motel."

Thatcher received these instructions meekly and decided to forgo explanations and apologies.

They were, he should have known, unnecessary.

"And the Checker Cab company called," Miss Corsa added. "It seems that you owe a Mr. Jerszy three dollars and seventy-five cents."

As intended, this caught him on the wing.

"Shall I send a check?"

"Please do," said Thatcher politely. Then, from motives that were not altogether admirable, he added: "And, Miss Corsa, let's not be stingy when it comes to the tip."

2

Over eighty years ago, a youthful Leonard Dreyer had ignored prudent advice and decided to sink every penny of his savings into a small factory in his home town of Roosendaal, New York. His venture succeeded beyond his wildest dreams. The Dreyer Chocolate Company grew from small beginnings to global fame. There were countries where the familiar gold bar had been more than a few ounces of chocolate; it had been a medium of exchange. At home no American reached the age of ten without having established a lifelong preference for the plain bar, the pecan bar, or the raisin bar. Soda fountains from Bangor to Buena Vista boasted pumps for Dreyer syrup and vats for Dreyer hot fudge. In millions of kitchens, hot chocolate was made with Dreyer cocoa, cookies were baked with Dreyer Tastibits, and layer cakes were enriched with Dreyer cooking chocolate.

By the time he died, full of years and honor, Leonard Dreyer had created his own monuments. First and foremost was the Dreyer Chocolate Company, itself—part industrial giant and part national landmark. Then there was the Leonard Dreyer Trust, to whose two-day meetings John Thatcher and others were hurrying. Finally there was Roosendaal, which duly recognized a *fait accompli* and became Dreyer, New York, "The Chocolate Capital of the World."

Like most of Wall Street, Thatcher had long been familiar with the company. It had a reputation for being financially sound and conservative to the point of stodginess. The thirty-five mile drive west from the Albany airport explained why it had nevertheless prospered. The rolling countryside was mellow with lush and abundant pasturage. At intervals signs for Amsterdam and Rotterdam Junction, for Canajoharie and Utica, testified to earlier inhabitants of this corner of upstate New York. In the land of James Fenimore Cooper, the Thruway along which they were speeding paralleled the old Mohawk Trail.

Finally they reached the Chocolate City itself. Everything was clean, neat, and prosperous. Far from being a grimy company town, Dreyer boasted a superabundance of parks, fountains, and playing fields. All these amenities, Thatcher feared, were about to become his responsibility. But there was no time to brood. He had barely deposited his belongings in the Royal Dutch Motel before the printed schedule demanded his presence in the Rembrandt Room for a business meeting of the Leonard Dreyer Trust.

Here he heard reports—from the director of the Dreyer Medical Institute, from the chairman of the Dreyer Center for the Performing Arts, from the curator of the

Dreyer Museum, from the conductor of the Dreyer Symphony. Between triumphs of the past and hopes for the future, Thatcher was introduced to the human element.

"Thatcher! We haven't had a chance to welcome you aboard. I want to introduce you to some people."

The man speaking was tall, gray-haired, and self-assured. It was only because his luxuriant black eyebrows had been a cartoonist's delight during his term of office that Thatcher was able to identify ex-governor Curtis Yeoman.

". . . and have you met Mrs. Ribblesdale? She's been on the board for two years."

While responding suitably, Thatcher was amused to note that Yeoman did not introduce himself. To the best of Thatcher's recollection they had never met, yet Yeoman was treating him like an old acquaintance. Exuding confidence, almost military in bearing, Curtis Yeoman simply assumed that everybody in Dreyer knew who he was. It was too early for character analysis, but Thatcher was willing to bet this was not the result of childish arrogance.

"And this is Reverend Buckner Chalmers, of the National Council of Christians and Jews," Yeoman was continuing relentlessly. "Bucky, this is John Thatcher from the Sloan Guaranty Trust. He's taking over from Bart Sims . . ."

Thatcher estimated that he met fifty people during cocktails. Over twenty of them were fellow trustees. But Yeoman showed no more tendency to linger over the distinguished senator and the Nobel laureate than over the musicologist and the choreographer. In fact, by gesture and intonation he was saying what old Bartlett Sims had put into words.

"Only three people are really important," he had harumphed before the Avis car had plowed into them. "The members of the steering committee. And that's Howard Vandevanter, Curtis Yeoman, and now you."

Considering that the function of the committee was to extract money from the company and then determine its apportionment, Thatcher was inclined to agree with this assessment. But Curtis Yeoman did not act like the member of a troika. He acted like a man who regarded himself—and was regarded by others—as first among his equals. Well, if he was expecting the man from the Sloan to be a deferential newcomer, he was in for a surprise.

But the evening was not far advanced before Thatcher discovered that Yeoman had a different casting in mind. The ex-governor had arranged for them to sit together during dinner and the interminable speeches that accompanied it.

"Thank God, that's over," Yeoman said briskly after the commissioner of Dreyer's Boys Town followed dessert. "Now we can get some more coffee. Oh, Vandevanter will thank us for coming and there'll be some informal chatting, but the heavy stuff is done. Waste of time, if you ask me."

"Everybody seems to have enjoyed it," said Thatcher although he had noticed enviously that the seat beside him remained vacant for the entire evening.

"Oh, it's all right for most of them," Yeoman admitted. "Some of them are really interested."

But men of affairs like us, he managed to imply, want to get our teeth into real problems.

"Tomorrow we'll be getting down to brass tacks with Vandevanter," he went on with a glint in his eye. "Our first priority is to get that dividend raised. Otherwise, all this talk isn't worth a damn."

"Oh?" At this stage of the game, Thatcher was not committing himself to anything. But he was beginning to wonder about the real reason for Bartlett Sims' retirement.

Yeoman grew too confidential. "I've been with the trust for twelve years now and I've gotten quite a lot accomplished. But I'm sorry to say that we're going to have trouble with Howard. You know that he's just been president since last May?"

Silently Thatcher nodded.

"In some ways I've been pleasantly surprised. At least

he's made one sensible decision—to start some advertising. And high time, too!"

For decades, Dreyer had operated on the theory that buying a Dreyer bar was a natural human instinct. But the recent decision to launch a new chocolate bar had finally led the company to Madison Avenue. In New York they were saying that Bridges, Gray & Kanelos were about to unveil a campaign designed to knock Coca-Cola, Geritol, and Gillette into a cocked hat.

"I'll hand Vandevanter that much," Yeoman admitted grudgingly. "But there's a lot more that needs doing. Basically, of course, the mistake was to choose a president whose expertise is so narrow. The only thing he's willing to concentrate on is the production and marketing of chocolate bars."

Picking his way with care, Thatcher suggested that was not inappropriate for the head of Dreyer.

"Oh, I'm not saying it isn't the right place to start. But we require more and, if he can't broaden his scope," Yeoman said, lowering his eyebrows threateningly, "it may turn out that he's not the man for the job."

Well, well, thought Thatcher, so that's the way the wind blows. It was not the newcomer from the Sloan who had to be kept in his place. It was the newcomer in the president's office.

"Just where is this broadening process supposed to begin?" he asked skeptically.

Curtis Yeoman was eager to tell him. "Right here!" he barked. "When a charitable trust holds most of a company's stock, you can't treat them like an ordinary shareholder. It's not as if they were interested in just money."

Thatcher reviewed some of his cocktail conversations. He had been acting as a trustee for scarcely six hours and already he had heard appeals for a radiological laboratory at the hospital, a revolving stage at the repertory theater, and a botanical expedition to South America for the arboretum.

"They seem quite interested in the things that money can buy," he said temperately.

Yeoman shifted his ground. "And then we have big and important operations which Howard doesn't begin to understand. I suppose you're going to say that Amory Shaw has New York under control—"

Thatcher, who was going to say no such thing, did not have to produce an alternative.

"Speak of the devil!"

The ruddy young man balancing his coffee cup at their side turned out to be Dick Frohlich, up from Dreyer's New York office. "I heard you mention Amory Shaw, Governor. He's the one I'm looking for. They told me he was sitting over here with you."

Yeoman was saying he did not know Shaw's whereabouts when Thatcher flicked the place card at the empty seat. "If this is your man, Frohlich, he never showed up this evening."

"Damn!" said Frohlich forcibly just as someone several seats down volunteered information.

"Amory phoned through before dinner to say he couldn't make it, Dick. But he'll be here in time for the meeting tomorrow."

This did not satisfy the burly young man. "Hell," he complained, "if I'd known he was staying in New York, I'd have stayed too. I've got to talk to him and his office said he was leaving early to fly up here."

So this was how everything in New York was under control, thought Thatcher. But Governor Yeoman moved promptly to prevent further disclosures.

"As long as you're here, Dick, why don't you join us for a minute. John is new to the steering committee and he's interested in . . ."

Looking preoccupied, Frohlich dropped heavily into the vacant chair. But he was basically a sociable young man and within minutes Yeoman had diverted him from his disappointment.

"You could say I work in New York, but mostly I

travel. I just got back from Ghana yesterday, as a matter of fact. Been looking over the crop . . ."

The sunburn, the rangy swing were explained. Dick Frohlich was one of Dreyer's roving cocoa buyers.

If Thatcher had a soft spot it was for experts, the more recondite the better. "Ghana's your chief source of supply for cocoa beans, isn't it?" he asked encouragingly.

"They produce about forty percent of the world crop," said Frohlich, warming despite himself. "The main crop will be coming in from now to about March. That's the biggest factor in the price Dreyer is going to have to pay for beans . . ."

Yeoman stirred restively but Frohlich kept his attention on Thatcher. "Of course, Dreyer uses a mix of beans," he said, folding powerful forearms on the table. "Next May and June I'll be checking on the midcrop output in Brazil. But Ghana's what really counts in our purchasing. Right now, most of the cocoa buyers in the world are padding around there, trying to second-guess the market."

Dick Frohlich's cheerful confidence made it clear that nobody was likely to second-guess him.

Tactful questioning elicited the fact that Frohlich had been buying cocoa for Dreyer for over fifteen years. "Funny how things turn out," he responded to interest from Thatcher. "I was a farm boy—but now I'd have a hard time telling wheat from oats."

But this was the extent of his philosophizing. He proceeded to give Thatcher a brisk rundown of world cocoa prices. Before he could complete his survey, clinking spoons indicated that Howard Vandevanter was about to make a few remarks.

The president of Dreyer, despite an unexpected shock of banana-yellow hair, was colorless in feature, voice, and expression. He was, however, succinct.

"First, I want to thank those of you who have contributed so much toward making this a banner year for the Leonard Dreyer Trust," he began. The mandatory tribute to the late Leonard Dreyer was covered in two sentences. Vandevanter wound up by pledging that the

Leonard Dreyer Trust and the Dreyer Chocolate Company would continue to reflect credit on their illustrious founder in the forthcoming year. Then, mercifully, he declared the meeting over.

In the confusion of general release, Yeoman made himself heard. "You may not be able to get hold of Amory Shaw tonight, Frohlich, but Vandevanter seems to be heading this way."

Frohlich turned to observe the conspicuous yellow head bearing down on them.

"Well, I'm not talking to him until I've seen Amory," he said more stubbornly than the circumstances warranted. "If you'll excuse me, I've got a poker game lined up back at the motel . . ."

He strode off before Vandevanter could reach them.

"That was Dick Frohlich, wasn't it?" Vandevanter said, looking after him curiously.

"Yes," said Yeoman. "For some reason he doesn't want to talk to you until he's seen Shaw."

Vandevanter's response was oblique.

"Well, both Frohlich and Amory will be meeting with us tomorrow," he said with a perfunctory smile that welcomed Thatcher to the steering committee. "I think you'll be interested . . ."

Thatcher knew exactly how to reply but Yeoman did not give him a chance.

"Where is Amory, anyway?" he demanded. "Frohlich sounded as if whatever he wants to talk about is pretty damned important."

This time Vandevanter convinced Thatcher he had taken Yeoman's measure. "Amory said something about not liking the look of the market, Curtis, so he decided to spend the afternoon in the office." Then he changed the subject: "Thatcher, have I described our new advertising campaign to you? Come along and meet . . ."

In the normal course of events there was little Thatcher wanted less than exposure to advertising campaigns. But, he had had enough of Curtis Yeoman for one day. And

21

Vandevanter had pointedly not included the governor in his invitation.

By the time Thatcher had exhaustively discussed Dreyer's sales plans with Vandevanter, and the Dreyer Animal Rescue Shelter with an animal lover whose name he did not catch, he decided to take a short stroll before bed and another round of meetings. Accordingly, he set out to walk back to the Royal Dutch Motel, through downtown Dreyer, which turned out to be a town that retired early.

When he arrived, Thatcher was careful to steer clear of the lobby. Only one importuning trustee, seeking a companionable nightcap, would be enough to scuttle his newfound serenity. Messages and phone calls, he decided, could wait until morning. So he proceeded directly through the parking lot toward the inner courtyard, where his own accommodations were located. In passing he noticed that not everybody was following his program. Convivial voices and low masculine laughter were filtering through a lighted window near the deserted dining room.

At the archway separating the two halves of the motel, he paused. Here, at least, no one was abroad. Patio lanterns provided the only illumination. Azalea and dogwood slumbered in the shadow and the swimming pool lay still and empty under a starry sky. A sliver of moon was setting over the dark hills in the distance. It was hard to believe that between himself and those hills lay the reality of a large industrial operation.

Tomorrow would produce more reality, in the form of facts and figures. Quite properly, Thatcher was prepared to defer judgment until he studied them. Nevertheless, despite the unreliability of first impressions, he was ending the day at Dreyer conscious of troublesome undercurrents.

Behind the lighted window, Dick Frohlich was less circumspect.

"Boy, that Yeoman is a nosy SOB!" Examining his

cards, he went on: "Every time I see him, he's pumping."

Sid Bousquet and Bob Reardon were still looking for openers while the two salesmen from Topeka were standing pat.

"Yeah . . ."

"Mm . . . mm . . ."

But once Reardon resumed his duties as dealer, Bousquet tore his attention from the two cards that were going to give him a flush. "Yeoman looking for any dirt he can find?"

"You're damned right he is. And he's got a nose for dirt."

For a while, the cards monopolized attention. Bob Reardon stuck with his tens and confidently eyed the pot through a round of amateurish bluffs. After he collected, he relaxed and said: "Something brewing between Shaw and Vandevanter, as usual?"

"Something's up," Frohlich agreed somberly. "But it's not the same as usual—believe me."

Reardon and Bousquet exchanged glances across Frohlich. They were all contemporaries but Frohlich's position kept him close to headquarters. He traveled around the world, true—but he reported to the top brass in Dreyer, as well as the top brass in New York. As a result, he knew and talked to people who were remote from Bob Reardon and Sid Bousquet.

"I've been trying to see Amory all day," Frohlich said moodily. He could not leave the subject alone.

Impatiently Bousquet said, "So you'll see him tomorrow. Probably he didn't want to leave the market today. They say Shaw's the smartest commodity man in the business."

"He's not as smart as he thinks," said Frohlich, picking up the deck and drilling cards around the table. "He acts like God Almighty, but he's sitting on a real pile of garbage down in New York."

Again there was a silent interchange between Reardon and Bousquet. This was one hell of a way to play poker.

Reardon decided to clear the air. "Say, Dick, what's the latest from Ghana? You just got back yesterday, didn't you?"

Frohlich reached for a new can of beer. "God, was it only yesterday? It seems like a million years ago—so much has happened since." He took a long drink, then the scowl returned and he grounded the can with a clatter. "But not enough. First thing tomorrow, I'm going to have it out with Amory Shaw. Whether he likes it or not."

But by tomorrow it was too late.

3

John Thatcher was sharing a breakfast table with Curtis Yeoman when he realized that something serious had happened. At first it seemed to be simply another count in Yeoman's indictment of the Royal Dutch Motel.

"I don't know what's come over this place," he grumbled. "It's never been the Ritz, but they've always been able to manage a simple breakfast."

The wrong table had been followed by the wrong juice. Now, he had been waiting fifteen minutes for a three-minute egg.

"There may be a crisis in the kitchen," said Thatcher, who could afford detachment. His grapefruit had been excellent and he was already halfway through his ham and eggs.

"There must be."

But Thatcher drew Yeoman's attention to an agitated cluster of waiters in the doorway.

"HOY!" Yeoman bellowed autocratically. "Hoy! You there . . ."

A flurried waiter approached and tried to apologize. "I'm sorry, sir . . . you see . . . that is . . ."

When Yeoman curtly demanded his eggs, he simply turned and fled.

"Ten to one, they'll be hardboiled!"

Thatcher ignored Yeoman to inspect the continuing conclave at the entrance.

"Whatever the dislocation is," he remarked, "I think it's bigger than the kitchen."

Yeoman's interest remained firmly centered on himself. "I don't want to make us late for this meeting with Vandevanter. You're going to get a real shock. You'll see that Amory Shaw is the only person at Dreyer who's really topnotch."

The arrival of overcooked eggs and cold toast put an end to Governor Yeoman's dogmatism. It also left Thatcher free to follow the agitation at the door. As he watched, the group broke up, with half of them hurrying out of sight.

"Disgraceful service, and I shall certainly complain to the manager."

But the manager was otherwise occupied, as they discovered when they finally put breakfast behind them. Wringing his hands, he was trotting through the lobby flanked by two uniformed policemen.

"Good God!" exclaimed Yeoman as the parade filed past him. "What's going on?"

He was officiously bent on finding out when his way was barred.

"We don't want people going into the courtyard right now," said one of the policemen.

While Yeoman expostulated, Thatcher questioned a nearby waiter.

"There's been an accident in the pool," he replied in an undertone.

Just then, a driver approached and announced that the car was waiting outside.

Gaping at fires and other tragedies had never held any

appeal for Thatcher. So he turned promptly to collect Yeoman for the short ride to Dreyer headquarters.

When they were ushered into the presidential suite ten minutes later, Howard Vandevanter was not there. The solitary occupant of the room was a tall bony man with thinning gray hair combed back from a high-domed forehead. He had a briefcase on his lap and was studying some documents.

"Hello, Amory," Yeoman greeted him. "Is Howard late again?"

Amory Shaw pulled an old-fashioned watch from an old-fashioned vest pocket. "You're early," he announced. "Howard had to take care of something. He'll be back in a few minutes."

Yeoman tried to improve on the idle moment. "You didn't miss much last night," he announced. "But I'm sorry we didn't have a chance to get together before this meeting."

Shaw was unresponsive. "I had to keep an eye on things in New York," he said.

Shaw might be repulsing Yeoman's overtures. Or he might simply be a man of few words. Thatcher could not tell.

In either case, Yeoman was undeterred. "I suppose you flew up first thing this morning."

"I got here late last night," Shaw corrected him.

Yeoman was overly casual as he said: "By the way, did Frohlich ever get in touch with you? There seems to be something happening down in New York—"

Shaw's voice was glacial. "No."

Curtis Yeoman was searching for a new gambit when the president of Dreyer finally arrived. Howard Vandevanter should have been a welcome relief, but he was not.

"This is terrible," he said without preamble. "Nothing like this has ever happened here before."

The blank incomprehension he saw made him swing toward Shaw.

"Didn't you tell them, Amory?"

Shaw was expressionless. "I thought you should break the bad news yourself."

"What bad news?" Yeoman asked sharply.

Vandevanter ran a hand through his bright hair. "Dick Frohlich is dead. He had an accident at the motel last night."

"At the motel?" Yeoman echoed. Then, as the implications began sinking in, he turned to stare speechlessly at Thatcher.

"Yes," Vandevanter continued. "That's why I thought you must already know. I've just been talking to the manager. He sounds as if they're all upset there."

"They're trying to keep it from the guests," Thatcher explained.

Doggedly Vandevanter continued with the details. "It seems Frohlich went to a wild party in one of the motel units. He must have gotten blind drunk, because on his way back to his own room, he fell into the pool. They found him early this morning—drowned."

This bald recital sparked a cross-examination.

"How could he fall into the pool?" Yeoman demanded. "It's lit at night—"

Vandevanter shrugged. "Well, that's what he did. He must have tried to go straight across the courtyard."

"You say he was drunk?" Shaw asked dubiously. "That doesn't sound like him."

"I've asked Reardon and Bousquet to come up here and explain," Vandevanter retorted. "They were there, too. But my God, the facts speak for themselves. Frohlich must have been stoned."

His reading was contested within fifteen minutes.

"Dick was not drunk," Bob Reardon insisted. He was haggard with shock.

"And we weren't having a brawl," Bousquet added abrasively. "We were playing poker."

Vandevanter waved this off. "It doesn't make much difference what you call it. You let Frohlich drink enough so he could kill himself. I can only thank God that he wasn't married."

But he did not get the cooperation he expected.

"Take a good look at us," Bousquet snapped back. "We're not feeling any too good. But only a damn fool would claim that we're hung over—"

Reardon was just as adamant. "For that matter, you can check with room service. We didn't have any hard liquor at all. Hell, we didn't leave the banquet until ten or ten-thirty. We played our last hand around one. In that time Dick had two or three beers. And everybody can tell you he was all right up at the hotel."

Thatcher felt bound to present his own evidence. "He was sober as a judge when he spoke with us, wouldn't you say, Yeoman?"

Support did not make Bousquet any less belligerent. "I wish to God I knew what did happen," he growled. "But I don't buy the drink story. And if you don't believe us, ask those two guys from Topeka. They'll bear us out."

The record was not going to show a drunken brawl, no matter what the president of Dreyer wanted.

"All right, all right," Vandevanter conceded. "Then he must have been sick. After all, he just got back from Ghana day before yesterday. Maybe he was running a fever, maybe he had a dizzy spell. But if he was sober, there must have been something wrong with him."

The poker players looked at each other. Reardon, Thatcher could see, was tempted to take the easy way out. But Bousquet's blood was up.

"He didn't look sick to me," he growled. "And if he was complaining, it wasn't about feeling lousy."

Reardon went further. "Dick was complaining about not being able to reach Mr. Shaw. Something about New York was bugging him."

"Do you know what it was?" Vandevanter got his question in seconds before Curtis Yeoman.

"No," said Reardon. "All I know is that Dick was steamed up about it. He left a couple of messages for Mr. Shaw . . ."

Throughout this exchange, Amory Shaw sat unmoved. His reaction when Vandevanter turned to him told

28

Thatcher a good deal about the independence of the New York office.

"I don't know what Frohlich wanted to talk to me about," Shaw said calmly. "I can't even guess at what it might have been. I have nothing to do with his operations."

Vandevanter did not dispute this. "Well, we'll probably never know now," he concluded. "Reardon and Bousquet have made things even more puzzling than they were before. It's all very unsatisfactory."

The situation grew even more unsatisfactory an hour later, when the police arrived.

Amory Shaw had barely begun his report when the chief of police demanded admission.

"I thought you'd want to know, Mr. Vandevanter."

"Of course, we're anxious to have this unfortunate accident cleared up, Captain Huggins. Frohlich was a valued and—"

The captain had no time for eulogies. "It wasn't any accident," he interrupted, silencing Vandevanter. "The doctor just told us. Frohlich was dead when he went into the pool."

"But that means—" Vandevanter broke off and began again. "You'd better tell us what you know, Captain."

"Frohlich got cracked over the head. I don't blame the men who hauled him out of the pool. They noticed it all right, but they assumed it had happened after he fell in. But now the doctor says different."

It is human nature to hope against hope.

"Isn't there any way it could have happened by accident?" Vandevanter was almost pleading.

Captain Huggins did not want a major scandal in Dreyer any more than the company did. Regretfully, he shook his head. "No, I didn't come here right away. My crew has been out at the motel for over an hour. There isn't any doubt at all. Frohlich was attacked in the shadows, just after he entered the second courtyard. We've located the spot where he fell into the bushes—there's still some blood there. Then the body got dumped into the pool. The killer hoped it would pass as an accident. Maybe he didn't realize that Frohlich was already dead and was counting on the pool to finish him off."

While Vandevanter stared, Governor Yeoman raised another possibility. "What about Frohlich's wallet? Was it missing?"

Thatcher could see that Captain Huggins had been over this ground himself. All he said, however, was: "No, we've ruled out robbery. It's early days yet, but we've got a couple of facts to go on. First off, it looks as if someone was waiting a while for Frohlich. Second, a couple of motels got calls last night—asking if Frohlich was registered. That adds up to a murderer tracking Frohlich down, then setting an ambush for him. He wasn't interested in anybody else."

There was nothing to say. The conclusion was inescapable. After waiting for objections, Huggins continued: "There's just one other thing. Frohlich was here in Dreyer for less than a day. We don't know much about him, and he was tied up at the banquet for most of the time. But it seems he was trying to get in touch with you—Mr. Shaw."

"So I understand," said Shaw stiffly.

Captain Huggins consulted mental notes. "He left a message at the office and he left a message at the motel desk. The young lady there says she gave it to you when you arrived at eleven."

Unhelpfully, Shaw waited for the direct question.

"Did you try to get in touch with Frohlich?" Huggins asked.

"No, I had had a long day and it was late. I decided to see him this morning."

The captain prodded further. "Frohlich told the desk it was very important."

This time Shaw was more forthcoming. "It may have been important to him, but it wasn't important to me. If I could have helped with his problem, I would have—but not in the middle of the night."

Vandevanter was frowning. "I didn't know you got into town last night, Amory."

"I don't know why you should have," said Amory, coolly. "I took the last plane to Albany, arriving at about ten. I rented a car and drove here. Then I checked in and"—his gesture was indefinably contemptuous—"and I went to my room, which was off the second courtyard of the Royal Dutch Motel."

"Yes, yes, Amory," Vandevanter said. "I didn't mean anything—"

But Shaw continued unhurriedly. "And I have no idea what Frohlich wanted to consult me about."

Captain Huggins had been content to let the president of Dreyer do his dirty work for him, but there were still questions to be put.

"Mr. Shaw," he said, "on that late plane last night, did you see anybody you knew? Anybody from Dreyer, I mean?"

Nobody liked the sound of this, least of all Amory Shaw. "I do not remember anyone," he said crisply. "The plane was unusually crowded."

They had strayed into Yeoman's political expertise. "The state legislature is in special session," he said knowledgeably. "All the planes to Albany must have been jammed. Anyway, are you thinking that somebody might have flown here—"

With more resignation than disappointment, Huggins said: "I forgot about the special session. You know, I'm beginning to wonder just how much we can do—up here in Dreyer."

He looked around, then deliberately and unmistakably spelled it all out: "Frohlich comes up from New York— and maybe his murderer does too. Frohlich is so worried that people can only remember one thing—he wanted to talk to Mr. Shaw. Well, whatever he was worried about happened in New York, didn't it? That's what we should be investigating, but it's outside my jurisdiction. Oh, we'll keep working here. With luck, we'll make some progress on the weapon and the getaway. But motive . . ." His voice died away and he shook his head ponderously. "If you ask me, that's down in New York."

Even allowing for a desire to pass the buck, this made sense. Thatcher was taken aback when Vandevanter implied that there might be protest from some quarters.

"Well, Amory," he said, neatly avoiding specifics, "you're in charge of Dreyer New York. In a way, you could say that it's really up to you."

Thatcher doubted whether Captain Huggins agreed. But the question was rendered moot.

Amory Shaw gave Vandevanter a humorless smile. "Yes," he said. "I quite agree. New York is the place to look."

4

In Dreyer, this was easy enough to say. But what about the other end? Thatcher could foresee strong, negative reactions from the personnel in Dreyer's New York office, let alone the overworked police force of that city.

But, since human nature is notoriously irrational, he was quite wrong. On the following Monday morning, two men were sitting in Dick Frohlich's office at Dreyer's Purchasing Division, on the fifth floor of the Cocoa Exchange. Neither of them was aggrieved. Overworked or not, Detective Dennis Udall was always curious about new worlds, and welcomed any opportunity to observe professionals pursuing strange occupations. His companion was more than eager to cooperate.

"Yes, that's right, I'm Stratton. I worked with Dick. God, of all the terrible things to happen—"

He broke off to shake his head. "Dick was a helluva nice guy. I hope you catch the bastard."

"You understand this is just a routine check. The people in Dreyer thought you could help fill in Frohlich's timetable last Thursday."

"Sure!" Stratton said mockingly. "It's so routine that the front office shot in two internal auditors last Friday. They put this place through a fine sieve over the weekend."

This was news to Udall. He tried to phrase his question tactfully. "And are they done?"

"Yes." Stratton smiled broadly. "We're clean as a whistle. Anybody who knew Dick could have told them that. He wouldn't have stood for any hanky-pank in this operation." Almost as an afterthought, he added: "Neither would I, as a matter of fact."

"And just for background, what is your operation here?"

Stratton was not the kind of expert who submerges any chance listener with a torrent of detail. "Couldn't be simpler. All we do is buy the cocoa beans that chocolate is made from. We go to the places where cocoa is grown, like Nigeria and Ghana. There are six of us in this office and together we buy over one hundred thousand tons of beans every year. You know Dick had just gotten back from Accra?"

"No. Does it make a difference?"

"It changes the routine a little. And, incidentally, it's another reason I was sure the auditors wouldn't find anything wrong. Dick had been away for over three weeks and he just hadn't been back long enough to stumble on anything. He landed at Kennedy on Wednesday evening."

"Did he check in here?"

"God, no, he would have been pooped. What with the jet trip and the time lag, you put in a twenty-hour day before you get to New York."

"So he probably went straight to bed?"

"You can bank on it. That's what we all do when we

33

get back from Africa. He didn't get into the office until about ten-thirty on Thursday and that's normal, too."

Udall was frowning thoughtfully. "Did you see Frohlich when he arrived on Thursday? What was he like?"

"I saw him actually come in the door," Stratton announced triumphantly, "and he was exactly the same as always. We yakked a little about his trip, but not much. Dick was awfully well organized. He made a habit of using the flight to get his notes in order. First thing, whenever he got back from a field trip, he sat down with a secretary and dictated his report so it could go straight up to Dreyer. That must have taken him about an hour and a half. The next bit was routine, too. Whenever any of us gets back from a cocoa field we drop in on Amory Shaw to tell him how things look."

"Wait a minute." Udall had been biding his time. "When I was down in the lobby I saw there were two Dreyer offices on the directory. There's this one on the fifth floor and one on the seventh. When I asked the elevator starter if the seventh floor was Mr. Frohlich's office, he acted as if I'd committed sacrilege and managed to say that the seventh floor was Mr. Amory Shaw. What gives?"

Stratton grinned. "For all practical purposes, you were spitting in church. We're ordinary mortals down here. But God lives on the seventh floor."

"You mean he's your boss?"

"We're not even that close to him. We're purchasing agents and we report to the vice-president in charge of production upstate. Our boss has thousands of people working for him and they all do something comprehensible. They take cocoa and sugar and milk and make it into chocolate. Amory Shaw is also a vice-president. He has one secretary, one assistant, and he spends his time buying and selling millions of dollars' worth of cocoa that doesn't exist."

But Stratton was playing games with the wrong man. The New York City Police Department had handpicked their emissary.

"You mean Shaw trades in futures on the Cocoa Exchange?" Udall asked politely.

"I prefer to think of it as black magic. Anyway, he's supposed to do it better than anyone else in the world. And one of the inputs he likes is our estimate about the upcoming cocoa crop. Dick went upstairs to see him about noon or so."

"And Frohlich would just give him agricultural information?"

"Not entirely. Basically we're experts on crop diseases, growing conditions, things like that. But Africa is Africa. We keep an ear to the ground for political trouble, too. After all, a revolution can do as much damage as an epidemic of black pod."

Detective Udall made some notes.

"So Frohlich went up to see Shaw. Do you have any idea what he did after that?"

"I can only guess. He was due upstate for the annual clambake, of course. They always have the buyer who's just come in from the field. If he was like me, he took his pay check to the bank. But I never saw him after noon on Thursday. I slipped out to a place across the street to watch television. By the time I got back Dick had already left."

Udall knew what had been on television last Thursday.

"The docking?" he asked.

"Yes. Wasn't it great? At first I thought they were going to blow it again. But when they finally linked up . . ."

Udall decided to leave. He had been the victim of too many space nuts down at headquarters not to recognize a man prepared to relive every glorious moment.

The seventh floor suite was much as Stratton had described it. Tucked into the end of a corridor, it could not have contained more than three rooms. In the outer office a shirt-sleeved young man was standing hunched over the typist.

"Look, Shirley, how many times do I have to tell you?

These columns should be in a line. They look like hell the way you set them up . . . Yes, what is it?"

Udall was not fooled for a minute. The young man had been conscious of a visitor from the first squeak of the door. Maybe he did want the columns aligned, but he was playing to the audience, too, putting over the role of dynamic executive demanding topnotch performance. Since Shirley was a good twenty years older than he was, she didn't like it one single bit.

"Are you Mr. Amory Shaw?"

Shirley snorted in derision.

"No," the young man snapped. "I'm Gene Orcutt, Mr. Shaw's assistant."

Anybody snapped at by Orcutt was a friend of Shirley's. "I'm Mrs. Macomber, Mr. Shaw's secretary." She beamed. "Mr. Shaw is down on the floor. Is there anything I can do?"

Udall identified himself and explained his interest in Dick Frohlich.

"Wasn't that just awful?" Shirley cried.

"Thursday, you say?" Orcutt frowned in deep thought. "Let me see . . ."

Mrs. Macomber did not give him a chance to perform. "Mr. Frohlich was here with Mr. Shaw just before lunch."

"Oh, yes," Orcutt said majestically. "He was telling us about the crop yields in Ghana."

Mrs. Macomber had other words for it. "He was reporting to Mr. Shaw."

Hostility between middle-aged secretaries and pompous young men is nothing new. It remained to be seen, thought Udall, if the cross fire could be turned to useful purposes.

"Do you remember what time Frohlich got here?" he asked impartially.

Orcutt guessed it was about noon.

"Could you get closer than that?"

Orcutt hemmed and hawed, said he knew it was before he went to lunch, and finally looked doubtfully at Shirley.

Mrs. Macomber studied the ceiling.

"I can't put a minute to it," Orcutt was saying when the door squeaked again.

As if by magic the two disputants disappeared, to be replaced by entirely different characters. Shirley, sitting four-square at her typewriter, was now the efficient secretary. Orcutt was the deferential subordinate advancing to receive commands.

"Any messages, Mrs. Macomber?" said the newcomer by way of greeting.

As the list was read, he trained a calm, dispassionate gaze on Udall. The total lack of curiosity was not arrogance, but assurance. If the visitor mattered, somebody would tell Amory Shaw who he was.

"Mr. Shaw," said Orcutt, eager to get in first, "this is Detective Udall from the police department. About Dick Frohlich—"

"Of course," said Shaw, nodding somberly to Udall. "You're checking on Dick's movements last Thursday. I saw him here around noon. Apparently he was looking for me later that day. But I went back onto the floor that afternoon. And I didn't get to Dreyer until later than I had planned. So I'm afraid I can't help you very much."

Without the slightest effort this lean, colorless man dominated his surroundings so effectively that all eyes were on him as he spoke.

"I would like to get a little closer on times, if possible," Udall persisted.

Shaw nodded, accepting the justice of the request. "I would say that he arrived at approximately twelve-fifteen. How long he stayed is more difficult. We talked for quite a while, I remember. Even after he had completed his report. Certainly nothing seemed to be troubling him. Now let me think . . ."

But when it was Mr. Shaw who required assistance, there was no nonsense about looking at the ceiling.

"Oh, Mr. Shaw, he was still with you when the docking

took place. And that was at exactly twelve-thirty-six," Shirley Macomber exclaimed.

Not to be outdone, young Orcutt made a contribution. "Yes," he said excitedly. "And you were both still in there when the American and Russian astronauts issued that joint message for universal brotherhood. I was here, listening to Shirley's radio and waiting for Frohlich to leave. Somebody will know the exact time of that, too."

Amory Shaw blinked at this outburst of enthusiasm from all sides. But he agreed with his assistants. "That's quite correct. The news of the docking came over the tape. And I remember that Dick was interested."

"What did he say?" asked Udall, largely to keep Shaw talking.

Shaw hesitated. "He made a pungent biological comparison," he said at last.

Udall suspected that in more unbuttoned surroundings Amory Shaw would have detailed the particulars of that comparison—but not with Mrs. Macomber and Gene Orcutt hanging on every word.

"Well, thank you very much, Mr. Shaw. I think that does tie it up. We can get the exact times from the news services. Would you say roughly twelve-fifteen to twelve-forty-five?"

"Yes. And I did phone in a few orders while Dick was with me. So if you have any trouble with the docking times, I could look those up for you."

"I'm sure that won't be necessary. But I would like to go over Frohlich's second visit."

"Certainly. Orcutt and Mrs. Macomber will do what they can to help you." Metaphorically Shaw's voice picked up his two assistants and cast them at Udall's feet. He himself turned for his own office, saying something about keeping up with the quotes.

"I was alone when Mr. Frohlich came the second time," Shirley volunteered. "He got here at two and asked for Mr. Shaw again. He was still here when Mr. Orcutt came back from lunch about five minutes later."

"That's right," said Orcutt hastily. "He was waiting in

Mr. Shaw's office. We talked for a few minutes, then he left. That's the last time I saw him."

Udall was still hoping that he was going to get a crack at Mrs. Macomber alone. "Frohlich didn't happen to mention where he had been, did he?" he asked, stalling for time.

"What? . . . Oh, no, no."

"He didn't tell me, but I know," said Mrs. Macomber creamily. "I happened to be talking to Jeanne Jesilko later. She said that Mr. Frohlich had been in to see Mr. Martini."

Orcutt was sticking like glue to Shirley's desk.

"Mr. Martini?" Udall asked resignedly.

Martini & Mears, Shirley informed him, was down the hall.

"Well, thank you," said Udall, snapping his notebook shut.

"Martini & Mears," read the legend on the frosted door. "Commodity Brokers."

Mr. Martini, the girl informed him, was on the floor.

"And when will he be back?"

"When the market closes," she said with an impudent twinkle. Then, relenting, she told him, "That's three o'clock."

Udall had a hunch. "Are you Jeanne Jesilko?" he asked and barely waited for her nod. "You free for lunch, Jeanne?"

She was sorry, she was meeting a friend.

As he had hoped, the friend was Shirley Macomber.

Russ Martini, commodity broker, proved to be a chunky balding man who moved with vigorous decision. He was riffling through a file of papers and giving directions to a miniskirted girl when Detective Udall finally got back to him.

". . . and check with the cashier . . . oh, yes, Mr. Udall. Jeanne said you were here earlier."

Just then, a head was stuck in the door.

"I'll be with you in a little while, Jim," said Martini. "This is the police, asking about last Thursday."

"Last Thursday!" said Jim with a groan. "Don't remind me. That was another Shaw Special."

"This is about Frohlich," explained Martini.

Jim sobered instantly. "God! What a helluva thing to happen! Well, do what you can, Russ."

"My partner," Martini identified the disappearing head. "Jim and I usually get together after the market closes. But anything I can do for you. As Jim says . . ."

A shrug and an eloquent palms-up gesture concluded the sentence.

"What's a Shaw Special?" Udall asked curiously.

Martini smiled. "When the market is slipping and everybody is waiting for the big buyers to come in, all eyes are on Amory Shaw. So he makes a big thing of not showing himself on the floor until he's ready to act. The tension can be quite a strain. Last Thursday Jim spent most of the day waiting for Amory. Ask anybody in cocoa about a Shaw Special."

"Thank you. Now I understand that Frohlich came by here last Thursday?"

Martini's smooth round head bobbed energetically. "That's right," he said. "Came in—oh, I'd say about one-thirty. We chewed the fat for a little, then cleaned up some loose ends in his account that had developed while he was out of the country. He left after about twenty minutes. He seemed the same as usual to me. I'm sorry I can't tell you anything else—or even be more specific. But things get pretty hectic around here, particularly during a Shaw Special . . ."

Udall was pleased at the way the times were slotting into the schedule.

"That's all right, sir. Now you say he had an account here?"

"Yes, he . . . excuse me . . ." Martini was already answering the phone. His side of the subsequent conversation was unintelligible to Udall although individual words were simple enough: *December contracts, hit the limit, delivery day.*

"Sorry," said Martini, writing furiously. "That's one of my biggest customers. He's crazy—but he can afford to be. Where was I? Oh, Dick. He took a little flyer every so often. I can show you his account if you want—"

"No, no," said Udall, rising to his feet. "That won't be necessary right now. In fact, we may not need it at all."

He did not add that future events might depend on the information he had already transmitted to headquarters, after a very successful luncheon for three.

"Frohlich was all right when he arrived. Oh, maybe he was a little tired, but he was calm enough. He just wanted to look over some of the day's buy orders," Shirley Macomber had said over her chef's salad. "Then that little snot Orcutt went into the office and closed the door behind him. Pretty soon the yelling started. Honest to God, it sounded to me like they were going to square off. That's why I'm so sure how long it lasted. I said to myself if it went on for over ten minutes, I was going to get some help. But even though they made plenty of noise, and every now and then somebody slammed something down, I couldn't make out what they were really saying. I'm sorry about that."

"Not half as sorry as I am," Udall told her.

"But before the ten minutes were up, Frohlich came storming out. He was really worked up by then. He stood by my desk for a while with his jaw kind of tight, getting himself under control. Then he said that it was absolutely urgent that he talk with Mr. Shaw as soon as possible. I didn't know then that Mr. Shaw would delay his flight to Dreyer. So I reminded Frohlich that they'd be meeting at the banquet. That seemed to relax him and he left."

Jeanne Jesilko emerged from her lasagna long enough to make one of her rare contributions to the conversation. "Then later on, when Mr. Shaw came back, you tried to get Mr. Frohlich."

"That's right," Shirley agreed. "I called the fifth floor and the girl there told me that Frohlich had left for the day. But I thought he might drop in on Mr. Martini. So I tried Jeanne. That's when I found out Frohlich had been there much earlier."

Udall tried to balance what he recognized as biased testimony. "But it boils down to the same thing, doesn't it? Frohlich came to your office at two o'clock in order to see Mr. Shaw. When he left, he still wanted to see Mr. Shaw."

"No." Shirley was very convincing. "When Frohlich came in, he was much more casual. It wasn't until after his fight with Orcutt that he was *burning* to see Mr. Shaw."

5

John Thatcher had been wrong about the response from Dick Frohlich's co-workers and the metropolitan police. His batting average was just as bad when it came to the larger financial world. He had not expected murder in an upstate motel to make waves on Wall Street. Dick Frohlich had not been a major force in American industry. His death would not trigger Senate hearings or solve the energy crisis. And these days that seemed to be all that people were talking about.

He discovered his error on Tuesday.

"It's Mr. Trinkam on the phone," announced Miss Corsa.

"John!" bawled Charlie. "Leo says you're not being very friendly. He tried to get you all day yesterday and you never returned his call."

"I didn't get back to the office from uptown," Thatcher defended himself as he thumbed through the messages on his spike. Good heavens! Leo Gilligan had called four times. "Why is he calling me? He's your client."

"He's the Sloan's client," said Charlie, sounding like Everett Gabler. "And I can't help him. He wants the inside dope on that murder you attended. He's here in my office now. Can you spare a couple of minutes?"

Thatcher agreed to come right along. Marching down the corridor, he tried to remember what he knew about Gilligan. As a special favor he had handled the account during Charlie's last vacation. Gilligan was one of Trinkam's favorite clients because . . . of course, that was it! Normally Charlie had to satisfy his taste for flamboyant personalities after hours. But Leo Gilligan was the exception. He was the financial buccaneer in Charlie's life. He had no use for carefully vetted blue chips and AAA bonds. Short-term treasuries left him cold. He did not believe in charts, in analysts, or even in price/earnings ratios. Leo Gilligan had made several fortunes as a commodity speculator.

Like termites, speculators do not enjoy general esteem. At regular intervals, they are excoriated by West German finance ministers and United States undersecretaries as enemies of basically sound structures. Besides their other nameless crimes, speculators are held responsible for the devaluation of the dollar, the pollution of the Mediterranean, and all British budgets since 1947.

At the Sloan Guaranty Trust such austere views did not obtain. No bank harbors a congenital aversion to the spectacle of money making money. All the same, Charlie Trinkam, financially conservative to his very marrow, followed Leo Gilligan's high-wire feats with awe.

In person Gilligan was a shrewd, thrusting little man who wore the kind of clothes most other men reserve for the country club. Today he was sporting a plaid vest and white spats.

He went straight to the point. "John, I hear you were up in Dreyer when Dick Frohlich was murdered."

"That's right," Thatcher admitted.

"You know how it is," said Gilligan. "Anything that

happens to Dreyer keeps the boys humming. Hell, when Amory Shaw sneezes . . ."

A roll of Gilligan's eyes told what happened at the New York Cocoa Exchange, and the London Cocoa Terminal Market, too, when Amory Shaw sneezed.

"Just like civil war in Nigeria," offered Charlie sagely.

Gilligan treated this seriously. Nodding, he said: "Only more so. Hell, all that business with the Ibos just confused half the guys down there! But everybody knows Amory. Russ Martini was saying just this morning . . ."

Gilligan, cluing Charlie in on what cocoa brokers were telling each other, was a talker. But his talk was not idle gossip. Gilligan made money because of one brute fact: the price of cocoa beans is set by supply and demand. As a result it goes up and, as so many people are chagrined to discover, it goes down.

Despite appearances, the essence of future trading is simple. If, like Dick Frohlich, you go to Ghana with a bulging wallet and buy a ton of beans, you have bought cocoa. The trade calls this the spot, or cash, market. Very few people are involved in it. The New York Cocoa Exchange exists to accommodate all the other people who want to buy contracts for cocoa several months in the future. The last thing Leo Gilligan wanted on his lawn in Darien was thirty thousand pounds of cocoa beans. It was those gyrating prices that engrossed his attention and kept him hopping. More specifically, it was the price that cocoa would be—next December.

If you enter into a contract to buy cocoa next December at eighty-seven cents a pound and the price rises until it finally reaches ninety-two cents, somebody will buy your interest and you have made a killing.

But what about the poor wretch who thought December prices would tumble? He has agreed to sell and, when December comes, he still has to deliver at eighty-seven. To put it in the language of the exchange, he takes a bath in cocoa. Or loses his shirt.

Of course the basic simplicity has thousands of ramifications. That contract for December delivery does not sit around in a drawer. People buy in and buy out many times every single day. And a customer may be involved in contracts with dozens of varying delivery dates. This is a futures exchange—a concourse of buyers and sellers, trading even more vigorously than people do on stock markets.

But while this dizzying activity might be meat and drink to Leo Gilligan, it was anathema to the Dreyer Chocolate Company. How can you plan the production of a ten-cent candy bar when inventory costs are bouncing around like so many Ping-Pong balls? So Dreyer is also forced into the futures market. As all commodity exchanges explain in glossy brochures, futures trading is not just an extension of Las Vegas. It is socially defensible because it enables Dreyer to shift the risk of cocoa price variations onto the shoulders of speculators. Thus Dreyer hedges against inventory loss and is free to concentrate on selling candy. In the textbooks, hedging is as good as speculating is bad.

Naturally, the perfect hedge that guarantees stabilization of costs is pure fantasy. Commodity users are happy to rack up any profits they can.

"And Amory Shaw has been making a mint for Dreyer longer than I can remember," said Leo Gilligan reverently.

"Well, he's got a built-in edge, doesn't he?" argued Charlie. "What Dreyer itself does affects the market."

"Oh sure. And with people like Dick Frohlich reporting to him, Amory knows more about the outlook than most. But still, he's got the real touch. He was born knowing when to stop."

Thatcher remembered the lean contained quality of Amory Shaw. "That could be native caution."

"No, Amory takes plenty of chances," Gilligan said stubbornly. "You know the old saying—be a bull, be a bear, but don't be a hog. That's Amory all over. And it's what's holding the New York cocoa market together at the moment. If anything's going to give, I'd like to know about it."

Thatcher replied that the newspaper accounts of Frohlich's death were substantially accurate. But, since banks serve their valued customers by passing on information, he added:

"There was one thing more. Frohlich seems to have been worried about something going on in the New York office."

Gilligan cocked his head. "That would be what he wanted to see Shaw about, I suppose," he murmured.

"You knew he wanted to see Shaw?" Thatcher could not remember that being mentioned in the *Times*. Indeed the account had been niggardly with the names of Dreyer personnel, in general.

"Dick told me so, himself," Gilligan said. "I bumped into him over at the Exchange on Thursday and he asked me if I knew where Shaw was. If you ask me, he was worried."

"Hindsight," Charlie suggested.

"We were all worried on Thursday," Gilligan replied. "We were waiting for Shaw to come on the floor and start buying. I don't think he plans these cliff-hangers on purpose. But he knows how to make himself felt. Sometimes he'll stand for days at the same place on the floor, just waiting. Some of the real suckers forget to watch the action, they're so busy watching Shaw."

It was clear that Leo Gilligan never made this mistake.

But Thatcher was gnawing on a different bone. How many people had known of Frohlich's determination to confront Shaw? He put the question to Gilligan.

"I heard Dick ask at least two other people for Shaw while I was on the way to a phone," Gilligan replied promptly.

Well, that settled that. Considering the way that gossip circulated at any exchange, Thatcher was now willing to bet that the entire cocoa fraternity had foreknowledge of Frohlich's quest.

"The real kicker," Gilligan said acutely, "is whether Dick was worried about his own office or Shaw's."

Thatcher said there was no evidence either way.

"I don't see how he could know anything about Shaw's office that Amory didn't know already," Gilligan mused. "Hell, that office is Amory!"

Gilligan was chewing his lip, wondering how this could affect cocoa prices. At last he sighed.

"It doesn't make sense. Not even that fight with Orcutt."

"Fight?" Charlie looked up hopefully. This sounded more like a murder. "And who's Orcutt?"

"You don't know about the fight?" Gilligan was astounded that this tidbit had not reached the Sloan. He gave them a synopsis. "The police are already onto it. They asked Orcutt where he was on Thursday night. He says he was home with his wife."

"Has anybody asked his wife?" Charlie, a lifelong bachelor, had patches of ignorance.

Gilligan scoffed. "Why bother? Hell, mine would alibi me if I'd gunned down the whole Exchange."

Thatcher did not like to deprive Charlie of insights into modern American marriage. But his own curiosity lay along different lines. "Does anybody know what the fight was about?"

"No, not even Russ Martini. He's my broker. And when Amory doesn't want to go on the floor himself, he uses Russ. So Martini knows the setup there. But what the hell! You can tangle with a guy without following him to the boonies and killing him. It isn't as if Orcutt knows anything. Amory plays his cards pretty close to the chest."

"All that means," Charlie pointed out, "is that Orcutt isn't supposed to know much."

Gilligan shook his head. "You don't know Amory Shaw."

"But I'd like to," Charlie said frankly. "Look, Leo, if you want to go over these accounts before you sign, why don't we do it at the Exchange? Who knows what will happen?"

"I can promise you Shaw, but I don't think I can go as far as another murder. Sure, come on. It's time you knew more about cocoa, anyway. That's what separates the men from the boys."

Charlie ignored this taunt, turning to Thatcher instead. "Coming, John? You might get your money's worth."

Thatcher declined. He had a client due in a few minutes. Somebody, he said virtuously, had to keep the Sloan running.

Charlie made a derisive noise.

"Are you dealing entirely in cocoa these days, Leo?" Thatcher asked. He could remember when corn and wheat had played some role in Gilligan's conversation.

"Pretty much. I like the action there," Gilligan replied.

It was a revealing preference. The New York Cocoa Exchange is even less regulated than other commodity exchanges. There are chaotic price swings, with thousands of dollars hanging on each quarter-cent fluctuation. Furthermore, since cocoa is traded in London several hours before New York opens, the real professional plugs currency spirals and arbitraging into his game plan.

"Cocoa," Gilligan summed up, "isn't for kids."

John Thatcher had been guilty of duplicity. True, a Sloan client was coming in. But the client had been handpicked. It had occurred to Thatcher that he was receiving too many aerial views of the Dreyer Company and its place in the sun. The Cocoa Exchange and Governor Curtis Yeoman were all very well in their way, but something less Olympian might be more useful. Something closer to a worm's eye view.

The Nagles were a survival from Thatcher's past. They had been one of his first independent accounts, many years ago. He had already seen one generation out. It was soon being explained to him that he was not going to ring in a third.

"That's why we're changing the voting stock," explained Fred Nagle shortly after entering with his wife, Helen. "I fought as long as I could. After all, we're the biggest candy jobbers in the Northeast corridor. You'd think my only son would want to come into the business. Where else will he find anything this good?"

"Fred, we've been all though that," his wife said wearily.

"I don't know what's gotten into Pete. Suddenly he says he can't stomach a lifetime of peddling chocolate bars. He makes it sound like heroin, or something."

"He didn't say that. All he said was—"

"I know what he said. To think that a son of mine . . ." Fred Nagle's voice cracked.

Thatcher had been through too many scenes like this. He wondered what young Pete Nagle's chosen alternative to Arrow Jobbers, Inc., would turn out to be. Thatcher had sympathized with fathers whose sons had joined communes, embraced Zen Buddhism, gone to the clink in Turkey, or were still seeking the perfect wave. What could it be this time?

Helen Nagle was the one who told him. "Pete has decided to be a veterinarian," she said, daring him to make something of it.

Once again Thatcher realized that he had confused a passing fad for a constant. The day of the guru was over. Was he now destined to hear a trail of fathers complain that their sons were settling down into pedestrian occupations, bringing home pay checks and supporting their families? Would mothers lament the absence of radical fire in their daughters? Only one thing was certain. If they did it anywhere, they would do it at the Sloan.

"I'm sorry that you're having this disappointment," Thatcher said, avoiding specifics, "but I understand that your son-in-law is active in the business."

"Him!"

"Now, Fred, you yourself admit that he's hard-working."

Further inquiry disclosed that the son-in-law was a

compendium of virtues. He was efficient, responsible, energetic, and even innovative.

"I just can't stand him, that's all," said Fred. Then, coming to his real grievance, he said: "And now Pete is going to go away and leave me with that jerk for the rest of my life."

Helen had had all she was going to take. "Well, Pete doesn't like him either. That's probably why he decided French poodles would be an improvement. Anyway, you don't see that much of Elroy. Not while you handle the buying and he does the selling."

Thatcher seized the moment.

"Then you're the one who deals with Dreyer, Fred?"

On subjects other than family, Fred Nagle was a rational man. "Sure," he said, shedding his melancholy. "I've been handling them since Dad retired. You remember that, John. It must have been twenty years ago."

"They're having their troubles right now. Have you read about it?"

"Troubles . . . oh, you mean they had some murder up there. I didn't pay much attention. It wasn't anyone we knew."

Murder at Dreyer did not cause the same tremors for a jobber as for a speculator. Personally Thatcher doubted if Fred Nagle would be alarmed until someone was pushed into a vat and wrapped as pecan bars.

"They've had some executive changes up there, too, haven't they?" Thatcher continued.

Fred needed no prompting on this topic. "That's right. There's this new president. At least he's heard about advertising. That's really all they need from where I stand. They've always been a good, reliable outfit, just like Hershey and Nestlé. Quality controls are first-rate, deliveries are handled the way they should be, the billing is systematic." He turned to his wife. "We've never had any trouble with them, have we?"

"No, and it isn't just us," she agreed. "I've never heard any wholesaler complain about them—except the deadbeats, of course."

Thatcher raised an inquiring eyebrow.

"Dreyer cuts you off pretty damn fast if you don't meet your bills," Fred Nagle amplified. "And they're right, too. There are too damn many fly-by-night outfits in this field. And nowadays a lot of them don't last—but they last long enough to rack up some sizable accounts if anybody's fool enough to give them credit."

At Arrow Jobbers bills were settled on the dot.

Helen didn't want Thatcher to think that Dreyer was heartless. "But they can be understanding, too, if there's a real reason to be slow in paying. You remember, Fred, when Dave Ingersoll died and so much of the estate was tied up, Dreyer let Irene go on for months. They even let her increase her orders."

Thatcher ticked over what he was hearing and singled out a fact new to him.

"I didn't realize there were so many failures among jobbers," he ventured. "I don't remember that."

"Ah," said Fred nostalgically. "Things have changed a lot since the days when you kept up with us, John. Sundries are killing the little man. We're all candy, tobacco, and sundry jobbers. Twenty years ago sundries meant pipe cleaners. Now you go crazy just trying to list them— ballpoint pens, sunglasses, combs, Alka-Seltzer, disposable lighters. And the biggest one of all!"

"What's that?" asked Thatcher, in danger of being swept off course.

"Batteries!" growled Fred. "Honest to God, I think people eat them. We can barely keep the stores stocked."

Helen was the one who could not be diverted. "And the great thing about Dreyer is the product. Because chocolate bars go on and on, while the fancy bars have their day and then fade. Except for the all-time greats, of course."

"Milky-Way," said Fred reverently.

"Baby Ruth," added Helen.

Not to be left out of things, Thatcher said, "Peanut butter cups."

His clients stared at him.

"My grandson eats them by the dozen," Thatcher said stoutly.

Fred waved away peanut butter cups. "That's just a stage kids go through. But all in all, Dreyer isn't a bad company. And now this new bar has pushed them into advertising, I've got no complaints. There's nothing like a healthy dose of publicity."

Thatcher was more cautious. "I'm afraid it depends on what kind, Fred. And now we'd better get down to the way you want to handle the preferred shares. I'm going to have to leave at three. I have an appointment uptown—with the president of Dreyer."

"Tell him," advised Fred, "that the sooner we see that new bar, the better."

6

As a matter of fact, Howard Vandevanter was already thinking about Dreyer's new candy bar. Old Glory had higher priority with him than the current meeting of the steering committee—which explained why he, Governor Yeoman, and John Thatcher were sitting in a small conference room at the advertising agency of Bridges, Gray & Kanelos.

Yeoman did not approve of makeshifts. Once the committee's work was done, his irritation overflowed. "Why drag us up here? Can't these people wait?"

Vandevanter met his complaints coolly. "I thought it was a convenient place for all of us. As for waiting, we're running out of time as it is. You should appreciate that, Curtis. You were all for Dreyer advertising, weren't you?

Our trucks will be delivering the first Old Glory bars to the jobbers tomorrow. You wouldn't want us to cancel out a week before our first TV spectacular, would you?"

"Of course not," Yeoman blustered.

Thatcher took refuge from this bickering by seizing a handy mock-up. It depicted animated Old Glory bars storming Fort Ticonderoga.

Vandevanter was relentless. "Well, someone has to think about the details, you know."

Predictably this did not silence Yeoman. "It shouldn't be the president of Dreyer. Not after your best cocoa buyer's been murdered. There are plenty of details there that could use some attention."

Vandevanter smiled. "You've reminded me of one," he said triumphantly. "I've arranged for us to run up and see Dick Frohlich's family. It shouldn't take too long."

Yeoman was no believer that sauce for the goose was sauce for the gander. "What? We don't have anything to do with company employment."

But Howard Vandevanter had him neatly hooked. "The personnel department is taking care of the formalities. But under the circumstances I thought we should make some formal expression of condolence." He looked at the ex-governor maliciously. "It is the least we can do."

"I thought Frohlich wasn't married," Thatcher objected.

"He wasn't," Vandevanter reassured him. "This is his sister. She and her husband came for the funeral and to start probate."

Yeoman relaxed once he realized that he was not going to be faced with a pathetic widow, but he made one last effort. "Maybe they'll be out," he suggested.

"They'll be in all afternoon," Vandevanter said firmly.

Thatcher decided that it would be quicker to satisfy Dreyer's president than to argue with him. So they were soon in a taxi speeding north. As the ride prolonged itself Thatcher began having doubts.

"Where are these people staying?" he asked at length. "In the suburbs?"

"No, they're in Frohlich's apartment. I think they're closing it up." Vandevanter peered out to examine a street sign. "It should be any minute now."

He was overly optimistic. Ten minutes more were required to complete a gigantic circle conforming to the latest one-way regulations. Then they halted before a luxury apartment house, where the security guard phoned their names upstairs.

"These are from Dreyer, too," he added.

This remark was explained when they arrived at a living room on the fourteenth floor. Waiting for them were a young married couple—and a familiar figure.

"Why, Amory!" exclaimed Vandevanter. "I didn't know you were coming."

"Mr. Shaw has been such a help," Eleanor Corwin explained after the introductions. "There were so many papers that seemed to be about Dick's business, and we didn't know what to do with them. In fact, I really don't know what to do about most of his things."

She looked around the room helplessly. There were signs of determined packing everywhere. Several large cartons had already been roped together and prominently labeled "Salvation Army." A large old-fashioned trunk, its lid open, stood in the middle of the floor revealing a portable typewriter and some photographic equipment. The table by Amory Shaw's chair supported an untidy heap of miscellaneous documents—brochures, printed reports, and typescript.

It was not the moment to add to the apartment's contents. Nevertheless Howard Vandevanter proffered the box he was carrying and said: "I thought you might like to have this. Dick's secretary went through his desk and put together his personal possessions. If I'd known you were having trouble with his files here, I could have sent her up to help you."

"That's all right. We're through the worst of it." Rodger Corwin was a lanky young man with a pleasant expression and ears that stuck out. He was also a compulsive host. He insisted on dispensing drinks although this operation taxed the resources of the small kitchenette. After rummaging through the cabinets, he finally produced six assorted glasses and a lone tray of ice.

While he was busy pouring, his wife had opened Vandevanter's box and was idly examining the clutter that accumulates in any office. She removed a fountain pen and an electric razor, some photographs, and a leather notebook. Finally she held aloft a large cheap pottery mug, with the remains of a gaudy legend.

"Oh dear," she murmured. "I didn't know Dick still had this." Suddenly she blinked, sniffed, and began to hunt wildly for a handkerchief.

With one accord, the men began a frenzied conversation.

"It's a good thing you were able to stay here," Thatcher heard himself saying inanely to Corwin. "Much more convenient, with all this work to do."

He was ably seconded. "Dick's lease doesn't run out for another five months," Rodger Corwin babbled back. "But the management already has a tenant lined up. What's more, they're willing to buy most of the furniture."

"That's good. Moving costs so much these days," said Curtis Yeoman, who was still living in the mansion in which he had been born, "that it's scarcely worthwhile."

"And you're from the Midwest, aren't you?" chimed in Vandevanter.

Rodger Corwin replied that they were from Green Bay, Wisconsin, and began a monologue on the many excellences of this community. Meanwhile muffled sounds from behind the handkerchief indicated that Dick Frohlich's sister was losing her battle. Finally she gave up and made a dash for the bathroom.

"I don't know what set Eleanor off," apologized her husband. "Actually we haven't seen that much of Dick for the last eight or ten years."

Everybody made sympathetic sounds. But with that

formality out of the way, Thatcher was not averse to a direct question.

"Then I suppose you didn't see him shortly before he died. The police are anxious to talk with anyone who did. He seems to have been upset about something."

Corwin shook his head regretfully. "Mr. Shaw asked me the same thing. But no, the last time I saw Dick was three or four months ago. I was in town on business and we had dinner. He seemed great, not worried about a thing."

Howard Vandevanter's gasp was audible. "Really, Amory," he said indignantly. "Bothering poor Mrs. Corwin at a time like this."

"It's a shame though, isn't it," Shaw said blandly. "Frohlich might have talked more freely to someone who wasn't from Dreyer."

"He certainly seems to have had his troubles with those who were," Vandevanter snapped. "What's all this I hear about Orcutt?"

Further hostilities were delayed by the return of Eleanor Corwin. Her face was shining clean and she was embarrassed.

"I'm so sorry. I never expected to break down like that. But it was the mug." She put out a forefinger and gently traced the remains of gold and red letters. "Dick and I got them when we were children. We sent in boxtops and used them to brush our teeth. I have no idea whatever happened to mine."

There was a moment's silence. Thatcher doubted if Eleanor Corwin was old enough to realize that she was saying good-by not only to a brother, but to her childhood as well.

Then she shook herself and deliberately changed the subject. "Oh, there was one other thing, Mr. Shaw. It came in the mail this morning and it seems to be about cocoa." She produced an envelope from the drawer of the writing table.

Shaw stood beside her, dwarfing her by his height, as he examined the enclosure.

"No," he said at last. "This isn't anything to do with us."

He was refolding the letter when Vandevanter interrupted. "What is it, Amory?" he asked sharply. "If it's about cocoa, it must be about Dreyer."

Shaw bristled at the tone, but handed over the envelope. Then he watched with sardonic amusement as Vandevanter frowned in puzzlement. When he finally spoke, it was as an instructor.

"That is a commodity broker's statement," he said slowly and distinctly. "It records a purchase of ten cocoa contracts."

Vandevanter's brow was still creased. "You mean Frohlich was trading on his own account?"

"That's right." Shaw turned again to Mrs. Corwin. "And the trade will make or lose money for the estate, depending on how the market goes. You should put this aside, with your brother's other financial papers, for the lawyer."

"But look here, Amory. This trade was made on the day of the murder." Vandevanter was too excited to watch his language and this was the first time that word had been used here. Its effect was immediate. Eleanor Corwin paled and Curtis Yeoman's lips folded together in disapproval. Thatcher noticed Rodger Corwin reach forward and press his wife's hand reassuringly.

Only Amory Shaw seemed not to notice the slip. "I don't see what difference that makes. Dick had just gotten back from Africa. It's natural that he'd want to look into his account and make a few changes."

Yeoman forestalled Vandevanter's reply. "Surely we can discuss this some other time, Howard," he said, his dramatic eyebrows semaphoring rebuke. "Mr. and Mrs. Corwin can't possibly be interested, and they're obviously very busy."

Vandevanter shot one horrified glance at his hostess and changed tack immediately. "Of course, of course." He made a curious ducking motion with his head and squared his shoulders.

The signs were familiar to Thatcher, who had seen them on all sorts of platforms. He reminded himself that, at least on the basis of precedent in Dreyer, Howard Vandevanter's public speeches were short and to the point.

"Mrs. Corwin, I have asked Governor Yeoman and Mr. Thatcher to accompany me today so that we could express the deep regret of the Leonard Dreyer Trust at the loss . . ."

One of the drawbacks to short speeches is that they do not allow the speaker to lose sight of his original preoccupation. Howard Vandevanter barely allowed Shaw time to settle in the taxi.

"That broker's statement was a complete surprise to me, Amory. I don't like the idea of Frohlich trading on his own account. And I still think the date may be—"

"Why don't you like it?" Shaw interrupted. He sounded amused.

"Good God! He had all sorts of inside information. It could have made difficulties."

Shaw was remorseless. "What difficulties?"

"How should I know?" Vandevanter exploded. "You're the expert on the Cocoa Exchange."

"Then if I'm the expert, listen to me. The only inside information Dick Frohlich had was his own forecast of the crop—exactly the same information he gave us. Dreyer dominates the market. Frohlich's trading was peanuts. He couldn't have affected our position at all."

Vandevanter hesitated. "I suppose there wouldn't have been any point in Frohlich's doctoring his reports to us?" he asked slowly.

"For Christ's sake!" Shaw made no attempt to hide his exasperation. "You saw the statement. It was a piddling trade for ten contracts. And Dick Frohlich had been our best cocoa buyer for years. You're talking slanderous nonsense, Howard."

By this time Thatcher was congratulating himself on having snaffled the front seat. No doubt Amory Shaw had reason on his side. Nevertheless, he seemed to be going out of his way to goad Vandevanter.

"I shouldn't have said that about Frohlich," Vandevanter conceded. "After all, he was the one who was murdered and he was the one who was worried about something in the New York office. Maybe he caught on to some fancy trading by one of the other buyers. I think we should get to the bottom of this."

"There's nothing to get to the bottom of," growled Shaw.

"Howard, you're making a mountain out of a molehill," said Curtis Yeoman, hurling himself into the fray. "We don't know that Frohlich's murder had anything to do with those remarks of his at that poker game. And the only trading we've seen is a small flyer."

Opposition simply made Vandevanter more obstinate.

"It wouldn't do any harm to circularize all our staff in the New York offices, asking them if they maintain private trading accounts," he argued. "At least that way we'd find out the extent of the problem."

"If that's all you want to know, you don't have to bother with any circularizing," Shaw retorted. "I can tell you. They all do."

"And you're satisfied with that? Why, if they were front-office executives dealing in company stock, they'd have to list every transaction for the SEC!"

"I know that. I'm a vice-president myself." Amory Shaw was very controlled. "The reason for that requirement is to protect stockholders in cases where executives might profit from inside information. This situation is entirely different. First of all, commodity exchanges aren't regulated the same way that stock exchanges are. Second of all, none of these boys have inside information in the sense you mean. It's safe to say that the only person who knows what position Dreyer is going to take on cocoa futures at any given moment is me. And even I don't know until I do it. It's all a matter of split-second timing."

Thatcher could see all too clearly the terrible abyss yawning ahead. In an attempt to keep Vandevanter from falling into it, he ventured a general comment. "The split-second timing seems to pay off."

"Dreyer's record on hedging is the best in the industry," Yeoman agreed at once.

Shaw smiled sourly. "And in case you're dying to ask, Howard, yes, I do trade on my own account. That is my third point—the custom of the trade. Everybody who has anything to do with commodities has something invested—stockboys, warehousemen, people at the Department of Agriculture. You have to accept that as a fact of life. But I'll tell you something else. In over thirty years, I have never put in my own order before the company's order."

Howard Vandevanter was in full retreat. First he had been forced to recant his suspicions of the dead man. Now he had to assert his faith in the head of Dreyer's New York office.

"Good God, Amory! Not for one moment was I suggesting any impropriety in your behavior. Your reputation speaks for itself. You've been Dreyer's trader as long as anyone can remember. I was merely pointing out the temptations that might exist for one of our younger, inexperienced men. Some of them are still on relatively small salaries and . . ."

His apologies and explanations lasted until the cab pulled up in front of the Sloan Guaranty Trust. Thatcher extracted himself, slammed the door, and waved his companions off. Only then did he realize with what expertise the president of Dreyer had been deflected from at least one of his discoveries.

Somehow they had all lost sight of the fact that Dick Frohlich's last trade had taken place on the same day as his murder.

7

Back at the Cocoa Exchange, meanwhile, Charlie Trinkam was unabashedly having a whale of a time. He had been delighted to meet the legendary Amory Shaw however briefly. Then he had offered to accompany Leo Gilligan on some errands. These too proved enlightening.

"Let me check with my brokers for a minute, Charlie. They're just down the hall from Dreyer," said Gilligan, heading for Martini & Mears.

"Be my guest," Charlie replied. He was here to get a feel for the cocoa world and this was one way to do it.

While Gilligan plunged into conversation with a thin, serious man, Charlie took Martini & Mears' measure: two desks for the principals, two secretaries, and eight telephones. It was very unassuming, yet Charlie knew many flossy operations uptown that did not handle half as much money as Martini & Mears.

Or a tenth as much paper work.

". . . but Mr. Martini, this is a refund check from the Hertz people. I don't understand how or where I'm supposed to enter it . . ."

The secretary's voice rang with every bookkeeper's exasperation over a misplaced entry. The rumble answering her was an indistinct baritone.

"But it's not a credit, Mr. Martini! And, it's made out to you personally, instead of Martini & Mears. So you see, I can't—"

Martini's voice and Martini himself reached Charlie simultaneously.

"Just give it to me, and forget all about it, Jeanne!" he was saying as he emerged into the waiting room. Jeanne was still mutinous but Martini settled the matter by plucking the offending check from her hand, jamming it into his pocket, then turning to Charlie.

"Hi," he said. "Anything I can do for you?"

Charlie explained that he was with Gilligan.

"Oh, is that Leo in with Jim?" Martini asked. "I want a word with him . . ."

Just then Gilligan appeared, trailed by Martini's partner. He and the two brokers put aside the minutiae of cocoa trading for more casual conversation with Charlie. But not for long.

"You know," Mears remarked, "it's a real shame. I was just telling Leo here. Poor Dick picked up a couple of thousand dollars in his account, while he was in Ghana. And now it won't do him any good."

There was a silent consensus that you can't take it with you.

"And it doesn't do Martini & Mears any good either, losing customers like that," Gilligan observed.

"If we had to live on commissions like Frohlich's, we'd starve to death," Martini said unsentimentally. "Speaking of which, I want to talk to you for a minute if you've got the time, Leo."

"Sure, go ahead," said Charlie when Gilligan looked inquiringly at him. "But I think I'll wait for you downstairs."

Martini and Gilligan were deep in the complexities of stop-loss orders before the door closed behind him. Even new-breed brokers, with their informal manners, are as inaccessible as the blue bloods of money management. Charlie knew better than to think that all the action was downstairs, on the Exchange floor. But that was where some action could be viewed.

At the public entrance to the Exchange there were the usual anonymous men, moving to and fro. There were strays with the unmistakable air of tourists—amateurs from Duluth and Seattle, come to see where their money came and went.

There was also a hairy sextet, brandishing movie cameras under the nose of a beleaguered official.

"The Exchange is closing," he was saying with bureaucratic precision, "in exactly twelve minutes. It is absolutely impossible . . ."

"Hold it!" said a bulky, bush-jacketed man modeled after Ernest Hemingway. "We need hours of time, not minutes. Glasscock promised us cooperation . . ."

"Cooperation?" the functionary squeaked. "It . . . is . . . utterly . . . out of the question . . . to keep the . . . Exchange . . . open . . . past . . . three . . . o'clock." He drew himself up. "Even for Public Broadcasting!"

In the ensuing chorus of protest, one of Ernest Hemingway's handmaidens turned and caught sight of Trinkam.

"Why, Charlie," she said, clanking in his direction. Barbaric hangings, chains, and twin curtains of cloudy hair momentarily thwarted his notable eye for women. Then, it came.

"Sonia," he said warmly.

"You recognize me?" She was disappointed.

"Anywhere," said Charlie, gallantly lying in his teeth. When last seen, Mrs. Sonia Libby had been wearing a mink coat, an Antigua tan, and a wedding ring worthy of Jason B. Libby, Industrial Real Estate. Now, with not a diamond in sight, Charlie prudently did not ask how Jason, and the children, were.

Nevertheless Sonia told him.

". . . happier now that I've cut out. I realized I wasn't a real person—only an empty, empty shell called wife and mother," she said, flaring her nostrils. "If I'd gone on, I would have been nothing. Now, I'm finding myself. And God, Charlie . . . !"

Charlie knew better than to encourage these dropout wives. He had a virtually inexhaustible interest in women but, of late, he had heard one too many explanations of how much better it was for the family when Mamma walked out.

"So, you decided to come to New York and get a job?" he inquired. By force of habit, he was escorting Sonia as she drifted after her companions.

"Craig is tremendous," she told him intensely. "Working with him . . . Well, Charlie, you can't begin to understand. He's so perceptive and sensitive. I didn't know what it is to *see* before I began working for him."

It rang a bell that coincided roughly with the buzzer signaling the end of trading on the New York Cocoa Exchange. As men streamed off the floor, Charlie placed Ernest Hemingway. Craig Phibbs was famous, in some circles, for his *cinéma vérité*. With a poetic camera and a disenchanted intelligence, he had produced the masterpieces that enabled Public Broadcasting to show how tawdry and commercial the rest of television was. Who could forget *Incest,* fifteen installments about life in parts of West Virginia that Jay Rockefeller would never see? Then, *Foetus,* the frank investigation-in-depth of the eighth pregnancy of an unwed mother. And what about *Suburb,* which showed Elmhurst, Illinois, for what it was?

". . . planning to call it *Greed*," Sonia was explaining while Phibbs looked around the Cocoa Exchange with curling lip. "Although some of us want to call it *Amerika.* That's with a *K.*"

Very few things surprised Charlie Trinkam, but this did. While not intimately acquainted with the personnel at the New York Cocoa Exchange, he would go bail that they were no different than the governors of the New York Stock Exchange, or the top brass at the Sloan Guaranty Trust. *They* would not be caught dead letting this cuckoo into their nests. He soon discovered he was underestimating the power of a woman clever enough to find herself without abandoning hearth and home.

"Eve Glasscock's husband runs this place," said Sonia, evincing contempt for Mrs. Glasscock, Mr. Glasscock, and the Cocoa Exchange. "But she's into educational television . . ."

"I see," said Charlie. Presumably time would improve Sonia's uncertain grasp of idiom. It was not easy, Charlie knew, to become an instant swinger after ten years amid the fallout of natural childbirth.

But at least the chain of command was explained. Mrs. Glasscock had nagged her husband into token submission. Glasscock then murmured something ambiguous about cooperation to his subordinates and got very, very busy. As a result, the hot potato came to rest in the hands of a man employed to give speeches to grammar schools, Girl Scouts, and church groups entitled "The Romance of Chocolate" or "From Africa to the Supermarket—Cocoa Beans in the Modern World." Mr. Clemence was probably the last man in the metropolitan area to use slides.

"Now this," he said, "is where cocoa futures are traded."

Six heads, plus Charlie's, swung obediently. Four or five men were clustered around the desk, where the details of the day's trades were being tallied.

Sonia and company were silent. Mr. Clemence inadvertently electrified them.

"Now here," he said, moving toward a circular table, "here is the pit. This is where bids and offers are made . . ."

But he had said the magic word.

"The pit," breathed Craig, falling into a trance. His acolytes excitedly chirped at each other:

". . . hours of coverage of the pit tomorrow . . ."

". . . catching faces . . ."

"No, Christopher, no! One face . . . one face throughout . . ."

Oblivious to the specter of Frank Norris, Mr. Clemence continued: "Now, when the market opens for trading, members of the Exchange come here. Orders are transmitted to them, by telephone or messenger, to buy or sell. When that happens, they go up to the pit and put in the orders. Sometimes, hand signals are used. Fingers vertically are quantity, fingers horizontally are price ..."

He had lost them again.

"Hand signals," said Craig Phibbs raptly. "Jesus, it's like mime!"

This time, Sonia hurled herself into the colloquy.

"... start with a still of Albrecht Dürer's praying hands ..."

"Marcel Marceau ... or maybe those shots of Frank Costello ..."

"... dead faces, with hands stabbing ..."

"We," said Craig, fixing burning eyes on Clemence, "are going to bring in our own lighting. With shadows ..."

Mr. Clemence looked at him. "Like hell you are," he said pleasantly, before continuing his discourse. "Now, over there are the observers, who are officials of the Exchange. They keep track of prices, time each transaction, then transmit them into the system ..."

To Charlie's growing satisfaction, there then ensued an example of the two cultures. Mr. Clemence simply carried on, describing the computer which fed receivers in brokerage offices from New York to San Francisco.

Craig, Sonia, and the rest of the Phibbsites plunged into communal ecstasy about tomorrow's footage. That men buying and selling cocoa futures would provide them with faces rivaling those of *Healing—A Week in a Hospital for the Criminally Insane,* they did not doubt. Neither did they doubt that they were going to dim lights, lower booms, and eavesdrop on any conversations going.

"I'm almost tempted to turn up here tomorrow," said Charlie, reluctantly preparing to tear himself away.

"Oh, you should," Sonia told him. "What Craig will focus on is one man, losing everything he's got in the world. Isn't that a tremendous idea? We'll show the hope, the fear in his eyes. We'll watch him trying to control himself. Then, we'll follow him home to his wife, his children ..."

"Great!" said Charlie heartily, storing this up for later use. "You mean, you want to catch a broker who's dealing for himself?"

Sonia's face projected more blankness than usual. "What do you mean?"

Across the room Craig Phibbs was also having difficulties. His deep, manly bellow brought quivering delight to his followers, including Sonia, who clutched Charlie's arm. "He's so real!"

Mr. Clemence did not seem to agree. "I simply said that not one single member of this exchange would allow you to listen in on his telephone conversations with his customers."

"Why not?" said Craig Phibbs with a significant smile.

"And," said Mr. Clemence, "before you barge into people's offices and photograph them, you're going to need a lot more than cooperation. You're going to need clearances. Frankly, if I were you, I'd check back with Mr. Glasscock."

A neater example of passing the buck back where it belonged, Charlie had rarely seen. Phibbs' eye for this sort of thing was not so sensitive. He was still expostulating when Charlie withdrew.

"Maybe we can get together for dinner some time," he said, without really thinking.

The new Sonia scorned anything but meaningful communication. "When?" she asked instantly.

Charlie took it like a man and made an engagement for the following week.

"Groovy," said Sonia. "I know a place that has really fine Nepalese food!"

Charlie Trinkam was deep in thought as he strolled into the lobby. For a good many years he had been a happy and contented man, thanks to the arts and skills he brought to his social life. But one thing was beginning to be obvious. The middle of a sexual revolution was no time for a man to rest on his laurels.

8

Characteristically, Charlie Trinkam was hit with a Nepalese restaurant at the Cocoa Exchange. Worse lay in store for John Thatcher the following day.

"You've got to drop everything and get right over here." Curtis Yeoman's phone call had been described as an emergency.

"Can't it wait? I'm in a committee meeting."

Yeoman was urgent. "Vandevanter's gone crazy."

"If I have to choose between devoting full time to the Sloan or to Dreyer," Thatcher said acidly, "you'd better find yourself a new trustee."

"Yes, yes," Yeoman agreed. "But you'll come this time, won't you?"

"All right," Thatcher grumbled.

Disengaging from the sixth floor of the Sloan was not easy. After Thatcher had saddled Charlie Trinkam with his committee, rescheduled another appointment, and survived Miss Corsa's frozen displeasure, he arrived at Amory Shaw's office gently simmering. But Curtis Yeoman cut him short.

"Amory's still on the floor, thank God! I need you to help calm him down when he comes off."

"You still haven't told me what the trouble is," Thatcher pointed out.

"You remember our trip downtown yesterday?"

"I am not likely to forget it." To date that taxi ride was Thatcher's chief grievance against the Leonard Dreyer Trust.

"Well, Howard thought over what Amory told him

68

about the custom of the trade. He decided it wouldn't do any good simply to ask the staff if they were dealing on their own account. His next bright idea was to insist on a full tabulation of cocoa trading from everyone employed in New York. Amory categorically refused. He said he wasn't handing twenty people an opportunity to show what brilliant fiction they could come up with. So Howard thought that one over, too."

Thatcher had come to rest with his hands planted on the back of a chair. "It sounds to me as if Vandevanter does too much thinking."

"Wait!" Yeoman held up a palm. "Listen to this. Howard has by-passed Amory. He's gone directly to the president of the Cocoa Exchange and he's demanding that the Exchange get statements from all brokers."

Thatcher circled the chair, sat in it, and studied the ceiling. Finally, he said: "What is Vandevanter after? Is he trying to force Shaw out?"

Before Yeoman could reply, the door opened to reveal a youthful figure.

"Shirley told me you were in here," it said. "Anything I can do for you?"

"That's all right," Yeoman said dismissively. "We're waiting for Shaw."

The young man stood his ground. "I'm afraid Mr. Shaw is on the floor, but I'm his assistant. If you tell me, I'll pass it on."

Yeoman shook his head. "We'll wait."

"Then I'll let him know as soon as he comes in."

"Thank you. The receptionist knows what to do," Yeoman growled to the closing door.

"Who was that?" Thatcher asked disapprovingly.

"Another one of Howard's brainstorms. As soon as he found out Amory was over sixty, he decided Dreyer needed a young man to learn the trade. You can imagine how enthusiastic Amory was."

Thatcher nodded. He was familiar with the problem of the senior man saddled with an assistant as a form of life insurance. It helps if these things can be done tactfully. "I suppose Shaw is dissatisfied with him."

"I don't think he pays much attention to Orcutt. Uses him as a general dogsbody and then ignores him. Anyway, Amory has always maintained that traders are born, not made."

"He may be right. Is this the Orcutt who had the quarrel with Frohlich?"

"Yes, but I doubt if it means much. Gene Orcutt has a good opinion of himself. He's always putting people's backs up. Do you hear what I hear? My God, somebody must have told Amory."

Amory Shaw listened in silence to Yeoman's narrative. Then he marched to the elevator and punched the button, undeterred by the fact that he was trailing two Dreyer trustees in his wake. In the presidential suite he returned no answer to the gentle patter of deferential greetings his appearance evoked. Instead he sailed directly toward target and threw open the inner door.

Three startled faces looked up. Howard Vandevanter and Russ Martini were flanking the desk but it was the man in between who heaved a sigh of relief.

"Amory! I'm glad you've come," he said, sincerity in every syllable. "We seem to have a little problem here . . ." His voice faded.

"I'll bet you do," said Shaw, showing his teeth.

Well, thought Thatcher philosophically, he had not expected it to be a cordial encounter.

Vandevanter took up the gauntlet. "I have been explaining my proposal to Mr. Glasscock. It occurred to me that the Exchange could solve all the difficulties you raised, Amory."

"Maybe we should all sit down and talk this over," the president of the Cocoa Exchange said weakly.

Even this innocent suggestion was not entirely successful. Thatcher and Yeoman were amenable. But Amory Shaw drifted over to a wall of bookshelves, set his back against it, folded his arms, and, looking down at the company from his great height, said: "I'll stay here."

Vandevanter plunged on. "I asked that Mr. Martini be present because I noticed he was the broker handling Frohlich's account. This way we can get the view of a broker without discussing the account of any existing Dreyer personnel."

Russ Martini looked hopefully toward the bookshelves but one glance convinced him that Shaw was saving his fire. He was going to have to take his own position. "I didn't know why Wayne Glasscock wanted me to come down here," he said, running a hand over his smooth, balding pate. "If I had known, I wouldn't have come. You can't ask me to dish up a lot of details about my customers. It wouldn't be long before I didn't have any customers."

"That's not what I meant at all, Mr. Martini." Vandevanter settled down to a job of persuasion. "Naturally, all brokers would have to cooperate. Then a customer would have no grounds for complaint. And there'd be no point in switching to another firm."

Martini was irritably fumbling for a cigarette. "If you ask me, there'd be plenty of point in switching out of cocoa futures if we started to play the game by these new rules."

"Oh, no." Vandevanter was earnest. "As Amory has explained to me, these people are trading because of their professional familiarity with this one commodity. Under those circumstances, they're not suddenly going to deal in something else."

"Brokers live on commissions, Mr. Vandevanter," Martini said bluntly. "And they're not chancing their livelihood on someone's theories."

Wayne Glasscock had been nodding to himself during this exchange. If the president of Dreyer wanted the reaction of a representative broker, he was getting it. Russ Martini could always be relied on to provide a dollop of sound common sense.

"I'm afraid that about sums it up," he said, trying to

sound regretful. "The practical difficulties make your proposal impossible, Mr. Vandevanter."

John Thatcher had often noticed that the men who make it all the way to the top usually have a little more tenacity than the general run of their colleagues.

"Horseshit!" snapped Vandevanter. "If we're going to review the practicalities, let's do it all the way. The customers we're talking about are all on the payroll of Dreyer and they're not going to be making any complaints. I'll see to that. And while we're at it, let me say that I don't like all these references to general procedures and what would happen if the Exchange did this every time somebody asked. You've got a lot of members who do nickel-and-dime business. But Dreyer has the most important seat on the Exchange. We damn near make the market. And we've got a right to ask for special consideration."

It was the moment Amory Shaw had been waiting for.

"Who did you say has that seat, Howard?" he asked silkily.

For a moment Vandevanter was confused. He had not expected his show of force to founder on a technicality. "Why, Dreyer . . . that is—"

"NO!" thundered Shaw. "I hold that seat."

Wayne Glasscock hurled himself into the breach. "As a matter of fact, the Cocoa Exchange prefers individual members."

Vandevanter received this instruction with poor grace. "All right, then, as a matter of form, the seat is in Amory's name."

"It's no formality," Shaw said icily. "I've held that seat for thirty years. For your information I held it before I worked for Dreyer. I'm the member of this Exchange, and I'm not making any idiotic proposals."

He was an impressive figure towering over the rest of them. Thatcher wondered if he realized that he was unconsciously assuming the stance he had made famous on the floor. There was a section of the wall down there known as Shaw's Rest and novice traders were warned off it. During frantic moments in the history of world cocoa he leaned there, impassive and immobile, while everyone waited to see how Dreyer would jump. Even the tweed jacket with leather patches that he wore for floor trading had become legendary. He was wearing it now. In a very real sense, this was Amory Shaw's ground on which they were fighting.

And Howard Vandevanter was growing aware of it. He abandoned the issue of the seat. "I don't understand your attitude, Amory," he said plaintively. "You ought to be on my side. Have you forgotten that Dick Frohlich was murdered? And we still don't know why. We can't simply let the situation drag on. And this is the only way to figure out what's been going on."

"A fine way!" jeered Shaw. "Throwing the whole Exchange into confusion."

"Then tell me a better way," Vandevanter challenged.

"I don't have to. My job isn't investigating murders. There's a big police force to do that. They won't have any trouble finding out about accounts they're interested in."

Russ Martini cleared his throat. "As a matter of fact, the police have already been around to my place. They wanted to see our records on Frohlich."

Vandevanter swung to the broker. "And you let them?"

"Sure." Martini stared at him. "What do you think I am? The police want to look at what a dead man has been up to, it's okay with me."

"Then why is it so impossible for Dreyer to do the same thing?"

Shaw intervened at once. "What Russ is saying politely is that the police have a legitimate interest. There is no indication that anybody else has. You have no right to start an investigation, even if that was what your proposal amounted to. And to me it sounds more like a fishing expedition."

"I see no reason why my good faith should be questioned." Howard Vandevanter flushed darkly.

"That's a remarkable statement from a man who has not hesitated to suggest that Dick Frohlich was double-dealing," Shaw flung back. "And you've come very close to making the same suggestion about me."

"You misunderstood me." Vandevanter did not sound apologetic. "And it is only natural that a few questions should be raised about a situation that has resulted in a murder."

"It depends on who asks the question, and why. So far, you're getting some very strange mileage out of this murder." Shaw raised his fingers and began ticking off the indictment. "You've seized the opportunity to cross-examine everyone in Frohlich's office. You've rattled Orcutt to the point where he's even more bumbling than usual. Now you're trying to use my seat on the Exchange to meddle in things you don't understand."

"I don't pretend to be a specialist about cocoa futures," Vandevanter said stiffly. "But I would remind you that your operation is part of the Dreyer Company."

Now Vandevanter, too, was on his feet and both antagonists were glowering at each other. They had eyes and ears for no one else.

Shaw smiled sardonically as he chose his words. "It's perfectly true that the New York office is part of Dreyer. But either I run my operation independently, or I don't run it at all."

"We'll see about that," Vandevanter said incautiously.

It was exactly what Shaw wanted.

"Then Dreyer will have to get along without one of us, won't it?" he said softly. "Would you like to bet which one it will be?"

9

The Dreyer Chocolate Company was one of *Fortune*'s Top Five Hundred. The New York Cocoa Exchange was nothing to sneeze at, either. But both edifices rested on the bedrock of customers shelling out for candy bars. A lot of people took this homely transaction more seriously than murder or the ominous break in cocoa prices that kept Amory Shaw glued to his desk the next day.

Among them was Fred Nagle, who had remembered John Thatcher's special interest in Dreyer.

". . . their advertising agency is Bridges, Gray & Kanelos. Kanelos is the one we're dealing with—Ted Kanelos. Although I understand his name is really Spiro—what's that, Helen? No, I am not bending John's ear with my prejudices. I am simply filling him in . . ."

Thatcher grinned at the long-suffering Miss Corsa. The dictation was going to have to wait until the end of this call.

"As I was saying," said Fred with the saintly resignation of one unjustly maligned, "we've been trying to help Kanelos find the perfect store. What's that, Helen? Oh, come on . . ."

Dispute resounded from the New Jersey warehouse of Arrow Jobbers, then a feminine voice took over. "John?"

"Hello, Helen," he replied. "You sound exasperated."

"Between Fred and Bridges, Gray & Kanelos, I defy anybody not to be exasperated," she retorted. "Has he explained how we got involved in the Old Glory promotion?"

Obviously, this was no time to nail Fred Nagle to the literal truth. In any event, Thatcher did know that Old Glory was in a Bridges, Gray & Kanelos countdown and that, somehow, Arrow Jobbers had been enlisted for the launch.

"Sure I told him," said Fred, who had found an extension. "And you're not claiming that I haven't been cooperating to the hilt, are you? I spent the whole morning showing Kanelos our humidity controls and the low-temperature rooms."

Arrow Jobbers' controlled atmosphere system, Thatcher had good reason to know, had cost three hundred thousand dollars. It was a masterpiece of sophisticated technology designed to keep cigars and cigarettes, as well as candy, absolutely virginal.

"Kanelos," Fred continued, "wouldn't care if we stocked Old Glory next to the furnace. All he wants is the ideal store—"

"Fred!" Helen protested on principle.

"Come on, Helen. Did he want to know about our biggest customers? No, he did not. When I told him about Sid's Fun Store in Times Square, he turned green. And what about New Era Variety, up in the Bronx? They're good for three—four thousand dollars in candy alone, week in, week out. And as for the stand at the Port Authority Bus Terminal! John, you should have seen his face!"

Helen tried to keep things from getting out of hand. "We don't want to waste John's time, do we? John, we wondered if you'd like to come out to Princeton with us—"

"I suppose it's inevitable that their ideal store should be in Princeton," he said, proving that he was just as bad as Fred.

"—to see the big kickoff for the Old Glory campaign," Helen finished firmly.

But while Thatcher could camouflage dereliction from

duty with the best of them, there was always Miss Corsa. Conscience can be assuaged, but not secretaries of her caliber. So, with true regret, he declined the tempting invitation.

Miss Corsa did not relax, and wisely so. Before ringing off, Thatcher solicited and received the promise of a detailed report.

When it came that evening, Fred Nagle had to admit that he could never do the day justice.

"Mr. Nagle! And, Mrs. Nagle, of course!" Ted Kanelos throbbed with gratitude. "You really did find the ideal store for us."

Modish in boots that gave him two critical inches, he surveyed the Corner Newspaper Store with profound approbation. The Corner Newspaper Store, in the person of its proprietors, saw things differently.

"Lordy!" said Ann Osler, unconsciously clinging to her husband. "Maybe we made a mistake, Mr. Nagle. Oh, it sounded fine when you called. But I never realized . . ."

Words failed her as Kanelos' staff began stripping candy boxes, racks of lighters, and displays of chewing gum from the space next to the cash register.

"Hold it!" Jack Osler commanded, removing a protective arm from Ann's shoulder. "I never said you could tear the place apart."

Kanelos intervened. "Don't worry about a thing! We'll put everything back. And just look at this . . ."

A complex merry-go-round was being assembled by skilled craftsmen, while aides, like nurses in an operating room, obeyed orders.

"Candy!"

Eager hands passed forward Old Glory bars to be inserted into miniature saddlebags.

"Flags!"

Small banners were dotted around the Dreyer-blue roof.

Then, at the flick of a switch, the merry-go-round magically came to life, twirling around and around to the cheery tinkle of "Yankee Doodle Dandy."

"The best goddam counter display in the whole goddam world. Hershey's doesn't have anything to touch it," proclaimed Ted Kanelos. "If that doesn't move Old Glory, nothing will."

Almost immediately, the test case materialized. A youthfully mature man cut his way through the crowd at the door with the skill born of his Sunday-morning forays in search of the *Times*. After deciding that none of the people inconveniencing him was part of a queue—they are not called lines in Princeton—he fetched up at the counter.

"Hi, Jack," he said, oblivious to Kanelos signaling for silence. "Let me have a pack of Luckies . . ."

While Osler turned, he idly studied the Dreyer merry-go-round. Then:

"Say, I nearly forgot! Take out for a quart of milk, too. I'll pick it up on the way out."

With Luckies in pocket, he made his way down the length of the store to the glass-paneled refrigerator. Returning, he waved at Jack Osler and drifted out. In other places, ten people holding their breath might make a dent. But, as Fred Nagle was to tell Thatcher later, that's Princeton for you.

"He's probably on a diet," said Kanelos, savagely. "Either that, or he's some kind of dummy!"

At this inopportune moment, Howard Vandevanter arrived.

"What's the matter?" he asked.

While Kanelos reassembled a strong confident smile, Ann Osler nipped in ahead of him. "Space is what's the matter," she declared, while her husband folded his arms and nodded. "People may give you some display space for Old Glory, but you can't expect them to put up anything as big as this!"

"She's right," Fred Nagle weighed in, reminding everybody that he was not a middleman for nothing. "Nine out of ten outlets are cramped—"

Kanelos was equipped with statistics on counterspaceadvertising expenditure ratios. Before he could open fire, there was another interruption.

A young mother, shepherding three small children and a beagle, elbowed Vandevanter out of her path. She planted herself at the counter while her offspring fanned down the aisles.

". . . *Newsweek, Vogue,* and *New Hampshire Profiles,*" said Jack Osler. "Two dollars and . . ."

But first totals were only rough estimates in Mrs. Keating's family. Tiny Ellen trotted up to her mother with an armload.

"Now, let's see . . ." said Mrs. Keating, in a show of enlightened parenthood. *"How to Know the Wildflowers.* Yes, Ellen, that's fine. Now what's this? *Let's Learn De-coupage.* Oh, Ellen, I'm afraid that's too grown-up . . ."

Ellen opened her perfect little mouth. "Aargh-gh-gh!"

"Maybe we'll take it," said Ellen's mother brightly.

David arrived with two bags of potato chips, three paperbacks about the New York Rangers, and *Popular Mechanics.* He was depositing them on the growing pile when Nicholas brought up the rear. Since he had located only a pictorial history of Scottish tartans, he was unsated. His predatory eye fell on the Dreyer merry-go-round.

"Wanna candy bar!"

"Oh, Nicholas!"

"Wanna candy bar!" Ellen knew a good thing when she heard one.

Only David remained quiet. He was marking time in sullen silence during the ten years between him and his driver's license.

Eighteen dollars and thirty cents later, Ellen, David, Nicholas, Samantha the beagle, and Mrs. Keating departed. For the first time in their lives, their serene assurance that the world loved them was right on the button.

"Five! Five Old Glory bars!" Ted Kanelos could have been announcing the Second Coming. "Folks, we've got a winner here. Old Glory is going to be an all-time block-buster."

No one, from Howard Vandevanter to the Oslers, had any desire to shoot this down.

"Now let's get cracking," said Kanelos, doing the trail boss to a T. "We've got a lot to do. Maurice . . ."

The merry-go-round was just the beginning. As conceived by Bridges, Gray & Kanelos, the Old Glory campaign was going to be multipronged. Dreyer was going to outdo matched Clydesdales and pastel airplanes.

His audience understood that, in this context, Kanelos meant one thing—television. Vandevanter, after all, had okayed a budget approximately twice as large as BBC's annual expenditures on all programming.

Looking impressed by the amounts named, Jack Osler said: "Boy, that's a lot of money. But I'll tell you one thing. Every time they put a new commercial on one of those kids' shows, we get troops of them in here asking for it."

"It certainly works for breakfast foods," Vandevanter agreed. "But it wasn't easy to convince the board. They've been selling Dreyer bars for years without any advertising . . ."

Before Jack Osler, Vandevanter, and her own husband could stray into shop talk about what a good, steady seller the Dreyer bar was, Helen Nagle forged ahead to another facet of Kanelos' grand strategy. Or, as he himself phrased it, the hearts-and-flowers bit.

Put simply, it was an attempt to capture the best of the old as well as the best of the new. "Sure, TV is essential," the Kanelos philosophy ran. "But let's not knock Norman Rockwell."

Norman Rockwell was not available. A lesser artist was. Moreover, he was waiting in the wings.

"His name is Maurice," said Helen to a frightened Ann Osler. "He's painted presidents and all sorts of people. Bridges, Gray & Kanelos commissioned him to do a series of scenes in a neighborhood store like yours, Ann. You know, people buying Old Glory bars."

Howard Vandevanter contributed his own endorsement. "We liked the idea at Dreyer because, after all,

we're not some Johnny-come-lately. Running these illus-
trations in magazines will underline what a fine old name
Dreyer has."

As he spoke, Helen Nagle sent her husband a look
worth volumes. All along she had claimed that Kanelos
was a smart cooky. It remained to be seen if he could sell
the great American public; he had certainly done a job on
the Dreyer Chocolate Company.

"So, that's why we've had this long search for your
store," she continued, seeing that both Oslers were still
lost. "They want something that's real, authentic—"

With a snort, Fred dismissed euphemism. "They want
something ideal."

Arrow Jobbers was picking up a fraction of the tab for
running local ads. This standard arrangement, plus an
unrivaled knowledge of candy vendors from Maine to
Maryland, explained why Fred Nagle was doing what he
could for Kanelos. Nothing could make him like it.

Kanelos brought his own brand of realism to the discussion. He began with a confession: "At first, I leaned
toward an older couple"—he flashed an ingratiating
smile—"just the way I was tempted by a New England
village, with a white church. I have my little weaknesses—
and besides, who wants to frame a portrait of the A&P?"

"The trouble with advertisers," said Maurice the artist
morosely, "is that they want all the kids to have red hair
and freckles."

Kanelos was touched on the raw. "Who said he wanted
this to be real—not hokey? Who said to cut the Tom
Sawyer kick? Who *knows* most little old ladies use
Clairol? Hell, I'm the one who writes the copy—not the
fathead who believes it! All I ask is that you skip the
gaping holes and the missing teeth. We're trying to peddle
candy bars—and every goddam dentist in the country is
against us!"

On this spasm of temper, he stalked over to the merry-
go-round.

Ann Osler was still daunted by the prospect of becoming a Dreyer pinup. "Maybe it would be better if you showed cows."

"Try telling Ted that," the artist advised glumly. "He'll tell you that nobody identifies with a cow."

Both Oslers were overwhelmed by the considerations, large and small, that go into a professional advertising pitch. Jack also had a more personal concern.

"Of course we like the place," he said looking around the Corner Newspaper Store as if seeing it for the first time. "But I'm not so sure anybody would want paintings of it."

The magazines and paperbacks lining the wall and central divider were neat enough. But there were cartons piled in the corners, out-of-date newspapers stacked for return, and that large, circular scanner that chills the innocent, if not the shoplifter.

"Trust me," beseeched Kanelos, reappearing. "And trust Maurice. You're ideal! The store's ideal—"

"And more important, Princeton customers are ideal too," Fred Nagle threw in.

Helen could see that Fred was cracking. Leaving Madison Avenue behind, she led him outdoors. Howard Vandevanter joined them.

"I know that a big advertising blowout has got to help put Old Glory over," Nagle told him. "But I never realized what a pain in the neck it would be."

Vandevanter nodded. "It was an eye-opener for me, too," he said. "And while we've got confidence in Kanelos, we want to supervise the way things are going."

"And how are things going?" Helen asked. The strategy of flattering womanly interest is age-old and virtually foolproof. To Helen's dismay, Vandevanter read too much into it.

"You know about Dick Frohlich's murder," he said. "God knows, it's been a nightmare. Everybody was shocked—up in Dreyer and here in New York. We're still trying to get back to normal . . ."

Helen, towed out of her depth, sent a silent SOS to her husband.

"It's one of those things that happen," he said with gruff directness. "Considering the thousands of people working for Dreyer, you could say that it's actually the law of averages. Accidents, crimes—they occur wherever you have more than two people."

Vandevanter could have been talking to himself. "You're probably right. But, my God, the way things are piling up doesn't look like the law of averages to me. First, there was Frohlich. That put all of us under a strain. God knows we've had front office squabbles before—but now they're turning into battles for survival. Then, on top of everything else, the price of cocoa cracked this morning."

Fred seized on the only innocuous subject in Vandevanter's discourse.

"It's got to be good for Dreyer, when the price of cocoa goes down, doesn't it?"

"Don't you believe it!" Vandevanter shot back. "Every unexpected change in cocoa prices creates a lot of problems for us. Our man at the Cocoa Exchange has his hands so full today that he's had to postpone a trip upstate." Vandevanter sounded obscurely pleased. "And it's made him mad as hell."

They had reached the Dreyer limousine. Here Vandevanter remembered to offer the Nagles a lift.

"No thanks," Fred lied without consulting Helen. "Our car's around the corner."

"Why didn't you take him up, Fred?" she asked once Vandevanter had swept away. "Do you really prefer going back with Kanelos?"

Fred had to think about his reply. "Kanelos may be a jerk, Helen. But right now, Vandevanter sounds like big trouble to me."

10

Howard Vandevanter had a looming television campaign and a collapsing cocoa market between Amory Shaw and himself. Gene Orcutt had no such protection. On the credit side of the ledger Shaw found his subordinate so distasteful that he rarely sought his company. But Orcutt would have had to be more than human to recognize this. Instead he was still pinning his faith on the deferential manner that had seen him through school, endeared him to his father-in-law, and caused the president of Dreyer to select him from a field of ten applicants.

Accordingly, when three o'clock signaled the close of trading, he bustled out of his own cubicle to lie in wait. An outsider, entering from the hall, would have observed an industrious young man searching through a pile of reports on the receptionist's desk. Although his jacket was off and his shirt sleeves rolled up, his collar was buttoned and his tie in place. Altogether he gave the impression of a tightly wrapped package with squared-off corners.

Mrs. Macomber was not deceived. "He won't be in a good mood," she warned.

Orcutt did not have to answer. The doorknob had already begun to turn. "The market's still sliding, I see," he sympathized as Shaw crossed the threshold.

"It only knows how to do two things. It either goes up or it goes down." Abruptly Shaw turned to the desk. "When Barnes calls, put him right through. Otherwise I don't want to be disturbed."

Other men might have taken this as a hint, but not Gene Orcutt. He followed Shaw into the inner office.

84

"Well?" barked his superior.

"Mr. Vandevanter was in a couple of hours ago," Orcutt began, before coming to a full stop.

Shaw did nothing to help him. He lowered himself into the swivel chair and let the silence prolong itself. Finally it was more than Orcutt could bear.

"He asked me a lot of questions about that last time Frohlich was here," he blurted. "He wanted to know what Frohlich said and why he was mad."

Amory Shaw reserved his criticism of Howard Vandevanter for his equals. "It's his company, he's got a right to know what's going on."

"But nothing's going on." Orcutt could hear his voice rising to a screech. He gulped and tried again. "I assured him that there wasn't any quarrel. Dick Frohlich was simply in a hurry and a little irritable. But Mr. Vandevanter doesn't pay attention to me. I thought if you told him . . ."

"How can I tell him anything?" Shaw asked. "I wasn't here."

"I didn't mean you could tell him what happened," Orcutt persisted, "but you could explain that we wouldn't be talking to each other about our private accounts. Because somehow Mr. Vandevanter has gotten the idea that's what it was all about."

Shaw had opened the humidor on his desk for the ritual cigar he allowed himself after the close of trading. Now he began to tap the cigar cutter against his fingernail, looking grimly amused.

"I suppose I could tell him that. After all, you never discuss your account with anyone, do you?"

Orcutt flushed. "I was given to understand that it was normal practice to have a private account."

"Oh, yes," Shaw agreed. "So normal that it's a common topic of conversation."

"I don't approve of that kind of gossip."

Amory Shaw's voice was like velvet. "Under certain circumstances, that is very understandable."

*   *   *

"Honest to God," Gene Orcutt said the moment he arrived home, "I don't think I can stand much more of that old bastard."

Over the last six months his wife had learned to read between the lines. "What's Mr. Shaw done now?" she asked, rushing forward with the cocktail shaker.

Meticulously Gene poured equal amounts into two glasses. At the same time he decided to censor the remarks following his unguarded exclamation.

"I think he's using the murder of Dick Frohlich to get me in bad with the front office, Betty," he said, when the moment for speech arrived.

"Oh!" Betty's dark eyes sparkled with indignation. "Just when everything was going so well."

Gene shook his head at the depravity of it all. "Of course, he'll do anything to hang on."

"I suppose he hasn't said anything about retiring?" Betty asked hopefully.

"Ha!" Gene snorted derisively. "Catch him retiring! He wants to die with his boots on."

He had started a new train of thought in Betty's mind. "My grandfather died at sixty-two," she said reflectively.

They both took a sip to celebrate this beautiful thought. But Gene Orcutt was not building castles in Spain.

"He looks sound as a bell to me," he said glumly.

His wife sighed but then looked for the sunny side. "Well, you know, we always thought you'd have to spend two or three years as his assistant. I know it's maddening the way he interferes with your work, but you'll feel better after our vacation."

"That's another thing. I'm sorry, honey, but we're going to have to scrub that trip to Sea Island. With Shaw trying to shaft me, I don't dare take the time off now." He reached forward to squeeze his wife's hand nervously.

"Not go! But we've already . . ." Then she conquered her disappointment. "It's so unfair, but I suppose you're right. You really think he might be up to something if you weren't there?"

Betty's position was clear. She still wanted to go to Sea Island, but she could be persuaded that it was not in their best interest.

Gene suppressed a sigh of relief. "There's just no telling. You see, I can convince Mr. Vandevanter that Shaw's talking through his hat, if I'm here. And, Mr. Vandevanter might be mad if I took off. You wouldn't know this, Betty, but the cocoa market's playing games right now."

Unconsciously Orcutt's chest expanded as he became the man of affairs he could not be in the office.

"You mean Dreyer has a lot at stake right now?" Betty asked humbly.

"Yes. The market can only go one of two ways. And somebody's got to keep an eye on Amory Shaw."

Like most brokers, Russ Martini wore two different hats. In the office he was a trader. Outside, he was a salesman. By preference he did most of his selling on the golf course near his home in Tarrytown. Today the late summer daylight was permitting him to try his hand on a local orthodontist.

"I don't recommend the commodity market to everyone, Talbott," he said gravely as they walked to the third green. "It's true you can make a killing. But you can also drop a bundle a lot faster than on the stock exchange."

Like most potential customers, Dr. Talbott was certain that heaven would steer him to the profits, not the losses.

"It's not just money," he said largely. "A lot of guys only want to build a portfolio. But I want excitement, too."

Martini considered this judiciously. "There is that, of course," he agreed at last. "And I grant you can get plenty of excitement out of commodities."

Over the years, Martini's pitch had been cunningly orchestrated to allow for teeing off, searching for lost balls, and blasting out of sand traps. Now he waited respectfully while Talbott chose his iron and transformed himself into a pillar of muscle. Then, when the mighty swing had been followed by a painful dribble down the fairway, he resumed.

"I suppose it boils down to a matter of temperament. Nervous anxious types are better off with something that moves at a slower pace, even if the profits are smaller." He cast an appraising glance at his companion and his companion's ball. "But the man who can ride with the punches, the man who can take a disappointment and come right back, he's a natural for commodities."

It was a shame, thought Russ Martini, that the ball had not sailed all the way to the green. He had the perfect sentence for that occasion, centering on the man with real drive, the man with a flair for hurdling obstacles. But if he didn't get a chance to use it on the third green, it was a cinch that he wasn't going to get any chance at all.

Dr. Talbott was proving his ability to come back fighting. It took him eight strokes to battle his way to the hole. Then, tossing the ball rhythmically, he mused: "It's funny to hear a broker trying to discourage a client."

"We have to be selective. A broker makes money out of successful customers," Martini said, skating lightly over the subject of commissions. "We figure that every new trader is going to take three or four falls at the start. Unless a client takes that into account, he's going to get discouraged and deal himself out. In my outfit we like to try for long-term relationships, where people know what they're getting into."

Here he seemed to lose interest in the conversation, turning his attention to the perils of the water hole. He knew that Dr. Talbott's internal dialogue would result in a decision before the sixth green. That would leave time in hand to thrash out remaining details before heading for the clubhouse. Martini always arranged things so that, by the time he was in the bar with a beer, there was no danger of other clients overhearing familiar phrases.

Today went precisely to schedule. By the sixth hole Dr. Talbott had decided that he was the man for these mountains. By the seventh, they were discussing which peak he would scale.

"I don't like the sound of pork bellies," he confessed.

This was the literal truth. At Martini & Mears they had long since come to grips with the fact that *wheat* and *platinum* are redolent of romance; pork bellies and frozen orange juice are totally devoid of magic.

By the eighth green, Dr. Talbott was fractiously rejecting all cereal grains. "I thought cocoa was where the action is," he said wistfully.

Their progress to the ninth hole was impeded by Russ Martini's lecture. Oh, yes, there was plenty of action in cocoa right now. Maybe, even, a little too much. A lot of people had gone short. Now the price was falling. And it would keep on falling until one of the big houses moved in to scoop the pool. Salvation was in the hands of one or two traders. Say Amory Shaw, he was the man who bought for Dreyer.

"Dreyer," Dr. Talbott breathed the name with a new reverence. "And when they buy, the price will go up?"

"Yes," said Martini soberly. "That's why everyone is watching Amory Shaw."

When Leo Gilligan had been a poor man, he occasionally tried selling things to other people. After he made his first million, the situation was reversed. But now he was in a different world entirely. All the nonsense about buying and selling had stopped. People expected him to give money away.

And, in the first years of plenty, Gilligan's donations had not been niggardly. But, he asked himself, was now the time to build a hospital wing damn-near single-handed?

"I'd have to think about that," he told his dinner host.

"It would mean so much to have your name—and Mrs. Gilligan's, of course—at the head of our list of pa-trons."

"I make it a point not to lend my name unless I'm willing to give adequate support to a cause," stalled Gilligan, trying to calculate how much this would cost.

"That's what we all admire so much about your contribution to local activities." The last thing the host wanted was the Gilligan name without the Gilligan check. He had hoped for a spontaneous, munificent suggestion. Now it looked as if specific sums would have to be bandied about. "The estimate for the new wing is three million dollars."

Gilligan smiled inscrutably. "A nice round sum," he remarked.

"Naturally we expect to raise a substantial portion by canvassing the community," his host said unrealistically.

"Sure."

Resentment descended on the host. Why had he been assured that Gilligan was an easy mark? He never would have made this approach except for the impressive list of previous Gilligan benefactions.

Gilligan got them both off the hook.

"Tell you what. We'd better let this whole thing ride a while. The cocoa market's going to hell right now. Makes it hard for me to say exactly where I stand. In a couple of weeks I'll know, one way or the other. That is," he added slyly, "if you can wait."

"Oh, we'll wait." The words came out too quickly. Returning to his urbane tone, the host blundered. "I didn't realize you were in difficulties."

Gilligan's face hardened. "I'm not in difficulties. I just don't have a lot of cash to throw around. But I can still pay my way." He looked contemptuously at the group gathered at the far end of the living room. "Better than most."

"Good Lord, I wasn't suggesting anything." What have I done? the host thought wildly. Can the man be going bankrupt? He tried to laugh. "It's hard for the rest of us to realize how you financiers work sometimes. Just put it down to our ignorance. I'm sure I wouldn't even understand how you're going to handle these . . . er . . . jitters on the cocoa market."

"I'm not going to handle them. Only one man can do that." Leo Gilligan pushed back his chair. "Shall we join the others?"

Amory Shaw had made it a lifelong habit not to let a solitary soul know his plans. He was fully aware that Gene Orcutt, Russ Martini, and Leo Gilligan—not to mention several hundred others—were all waiting to see which way he would jump. In the privacy of his apartment he finished his review of the papers before him, and decided to let them all wait.

"No, not tomorrow," he murmured. "That would be too early."

11

Sophisticated techniques do not fundamentally alter human communication. They simply accelerate it past the speed of sound. No one's voice can keep pace with telex and computer. As a result, time is even more relative on Wall Street than elsewhere.

"Today's the day," said the caller on the phone the following afternoon.

Miss Corsa had already identified Howard Vandevanter. Nevertheless Thatcher found it hard to slow down to the Dreyer Chocolate Company's tempo. In the past six hours he and the rest of the stock exchange had lived through several days.

First, before the market opened, came rumors from Beverly Hills and the State of Illinois. Then, like ice breaking up in the Yukon, debris floated downstream. By midmorning, everybody knew: giant, high-flying Union Funding was in trouble. And, even before senior partners at venerable accounting firms and mutual funds could pull themselves together for guarded statements, proof came tumbling down the chute: forged paper, falsified policies, doctored books.

They were crooks at Union Funding.

The Sloan Guaranty Trust had always suspected as much.

"Say what you want," Walter Bowman, the bank's chief of research, had put it many months ago, "who needs swingers, when you're talking about reinsurance? Besides, you know that rate of growth people keep talking about? They do it by revising last year's figures downward, regular as rain."

So, the Sloan was not directly involved in the cataclysm. But the Sloan and Thatcher were involved with many grave, conservative men who did business with Union Funding, who had invested millions of dollars in Union Funding, who were now consulting their grave, conservative lawyers about Union Funding. When a mighty oak crashes there may be stillness in the forest, but not on Wall Street.

"Some of the biggest names on the Street are getting caught," indignantly reported Tom Robichaux, of Robichaux & Devane.

"Well, if that makes you feel better," said Thatcher with the frankness of an old friend.

"Better, hell!" said Robichaux stoutly. "You know what the SOBs are doing? They're refusing to take delivery from us!"

Big names do not like getting stung any better than anyone else. Thatcher had heard from a lot of them by the time Miss Corsa put Vandevanter through. It was not easy to veer from lawsuits, rigged computers, and SEC investigations to candy bars.

". . . talked to Curtis Yeoman, who's fortunately still in town," Vandevanter was saying.

"Sorry, I missed that," said Thatcher simultaneously scanning the note Miss Corsa handed him; consent decrees and incredulity in Los Angeles, New York, and Chicago.

Vandevanter grew impatient. "Tonight's the night we're officially launching the advertising campaign for Old Glory. Kanelos had an idea and, as I say, I've already spoken to Yeoman about it. This afternoon, we're going to release a brief statement to the trade . . ."

Thatcher would have had no compunction about refusing to lend himself to the Dreyer Chocolate Company's promotional efforts. Financial advice, not a warm body, was what he had agreed to contribute to the Leonard Dreyer Trust. But just then, Charlie Trinkam stuck his head in the door, his face alight with unholy glee.

"Silverman's suing Robichaux & Devane! And Stose claims it didn't have inside information. It was pure coincidence they unloaded Union Funding yesterday!"

That made up Thatcher's mind. When big names began turning on big names, he preferred to be elsewhere. Particularly after another face appeared over Charlie's shoulder.

"Market's down twenty-three," said Walter Bowman. "That damned nitwit up in Boston calls it a crisis in confidence."

Thatcher was an old hand at riding out storms. After lengthy instructions to subordinates, he safeguarded himself by leaving.

Very few people ever stepped so springily from the frying pan into the fire.

Curtis Yeoman was waiting for him in the lobby of the Cocoa Exchange.

"I understand that the price of cocoa is still sinking," he said with the detachment of a neutral. He did not bother to lower his voice, so his words were audible to everybody in the vicinity.

"We'd better be getting upstairs," said Thatcher hurriedly. With cocoa futures hitting the lower limit day after day, Yeoman's tourist approach was about as welcome as stray bird watchers would have been during the battle of Little Big Horn.

Thatcher had hustled Yeoman into an elevator when they were hailed.

"Come to watch us bleed, Thatcher?"

"Hello, Gilligan," Thatcher replied temperately. "Have you met Governor Yeoman, here?"

Thatcher planned confining himself to introductions, but Yeoman had less sense. "Pretty exciting time for you cocoa people," he remarked with tactless geniality.

Gilligan regarded him sourly. "Oh, it's exciting all right—like jumping off a cliff."

"How do you read the rest of the day, Gilligan?" Thatcher asked, although there was little he wanted less to know. The last hour of trading always makes bad situations worse. But he felt morally bound to intervene. Flesh and blood can stand so much, and men battered by selling waves should not be asked for small talk on the subject. This, incidentally, was a point ignored by too many Wall Street wives, as witness the divorce rate among customers' men.

"It all depends on Amory," Gilligan said harshly. "We're waiting for him—just the way we waited all day yesterday."

"You mean he hasn't acted yet?" Yeoman asked.

Gilligan replied: "The whole damned market thought Amory had to move in yesterday. But he just went down, watched—then left. Then this morning—the same thing!"

The doors oozed open on the fifth floor.

"So now," said Gilligan before they stepped out, "I'm going on up to ask Russ when the hell he thinks Amory is going to do something. He's got Jim down on the floor to spell him while he checks around. But hell, I know what he's going to tell me. He knows as much about Amory as the rest of us."

When they were alone, Yeoman's curiosity overflowed. He proved startlingly ignorant about the realities of cocoa trading.

"Everybody here is waiting for Dreyer to start buying, to put some support into this market," Thatcher was explaining as they turned the corner.

"You can say that again!" The fervent statement came from a total stranger passing by. "Is Amory down on the floor now?"

Thatcher replied that he did not know.

"No, he's just left," said a second stranger, coming toward them. "Didn't do anything, just stood there."

"Je-*sus!*" said Thatcher's stranger, scuttling off.

"Good God!" Yeoman exclaimed. "I hadn't realized the atmosphere down here at all!"

It had its appeal too, Thatcher could see, but a more humdrum world beckoned from beyond the door: *Dreyer Cocoa Purchasing Division*. They had not yet made certain necessary changes. There, halfway down a list of names, was—*R. Frohlich*.

Thatcher wondered if Curtis Yeoman too had noticed.

". . . one of the most dramatic developments in Dreyer's history!" Mr. Kanelos was already on stage when Thatcher and Yeoman let themselves in. "The Old Glory bar—the finest ten-cent candy bar in American history, and in view of today's prices, the best bargain the American consumer can get . . ."

Eight or ten representatives of the trade and financial press, profoundly bored, studied the press release and jotted desultory notes.

". . . for a few words, the president of the Dreyer Chocolate Company, Mr. Howard Vandevanter . . ."

Vandevanter blinked, cleared his throat, and opened his remarks. Thatcher listened with half an ear. There was no reason for Dreyer to have a Demosthenes at the helm, but why did Vandevanter always manage to sound like a civil engineer?

". . . addition to our line of quality products," he read without inflection.

Outside, the turbulent cocoa market churned unnoticed, except presumably by Amory Shaw, whose absence did not surprise Thatcher.

". . . a landmark for the Dreyer Chocolate Company. And, as many of you know, for another organization, the Leonard Dreyer Trust. This afternoon two trustees are present and I am going to call upon them . . ."

Thatcher decided he could safely leave this one to Yeoman. After an initial grunt of outrage the ex-governor let fly with a short, combative response. After the mandatory good wishes, he delivered the warning that should have been unnecessary: any mention of the Leonard Dreyer Trust in connection with commercial promotion of Old Glory would be regarded by the trustees as actionable.

With that, he sat down.

"Irresponsible idiots," he said aloud.

Thatcher foresaw a session designed to teach Bridges, Gray & Kanelos that it never pays to underestimate the power of a tax-exempt status. It would not be the first time that the optimism and joviality of the press conference held up only until the last reporter left. But the battle royal Thatcher expected after *Chocolate News* departed never got off the ground.

"Where's Amory?" Vandevanter was so preoccupied that he ignored Yeoman's bristling approach.

"How do I know?" Yeoman shot back. "Howard, I want to talk—"

But he was not in a one-on-one confrontation. There was a goodly array of Dreyer small fry present, and they knew which questions to answer.

". . . down on the floor, I believe, sir . . ."

". . . call Mrs. Macomber, his secretary . . ."

". . . looked in his office upstairs before I came down . . ."

Yeoman could have held his own against the medley of

respectful voices if Vandevanter had not singled out the last of them:

"You're Orcutt, aren't you? Are you saying you don't know where Shaw is?"

Gene Orcutt reddened under Vandevanter's accusation but kept his composure.

"Mr. Shaw's been up and down to the floor all day, Mr. Vandevanter. He's keeping a minute-to-minute watch on what's happening."

"I know that!" Vandevanter would have continued, but his attention was claimed by Ted Kanelos.

"I think we should be getting over to the studio," Kanelos started when Vandevanter cut him short.

"You go on ahead, Kanelos. I'm going to be busy here for a while. Orcutt, see if you can locate Shaw, will you? I want to see him for a few minutes . . ."

Thatcher, who had not budged from his roost in the audience, was unimpressed by the performance. The supporting players were all right: Kanelos, hurrying out to important appointments; Orcutt, nodding vigorously and saying, "Right! . . . right!" Even the spear carriers listened to the president of the Dreyer Chocolate Company with energy. But Howard Vandevanter as clipped, dynamic executive was miscast.

Yeoman, on the other hand, was exhibiting more self-control than Thatcher would have credited him with.

"Vandevanter, we're going to have this out—about using the Trust!"

Vandevanter broke off his conversation with Orcutt. "Oh, Yeoman," he said vaguely. "I'm afraid I'm a little too busy right now . . ."

With that, he moved to the door through which Kanelos had disappeared, buffered by the entourage which automatically grouped around him.

This left Thatcher with Governor Yeoman, and young Orcutt.

Orcutt, moodily chewing his underlip, looked ready to burst into speech. But, after a quick appraisal of Yeoman and Thatcher, he darted out after Vandevanter.

Yeoman had to vent his emotions. "Did you see that!" he roared, white with fury. "Who the hell does Vandevanter think he is? If he thinks . . ."

Thatcher made no effort to dam the flood. Right now, only one of the woolier saints would try peacemaking.

"Well, if he thinks he's getting away with it," Yeoman growled, "he's got bats in the belfry! Are you coming with me?"

"No!"

This monosyllable halted Yeoman's determined progress to the door only briefly. But, after a half-beat of blank curiosity, anger overtook him again.

"Suit yourself," he said curtly, striding out.

So much for setting a good example, thought Thatcher, taking his time about leaving Dreyer's Cocoa Purchasing Division. Downstairs, millions of dollars hung in the balance, waiting on Amory Shaw. Upstairs, a whole gang of people were stalking each other.

When he reached street level, Thatcher let impulse lead him around the corner to the public entrance of the Cocoa Exchange. The visitors' gallery was a minuscule perch hung only feet above the floor, not a remote, glass-encased viewing post. The circular trading table was the focus of a modest room, not a vast cavern. The clerk at the desk could have yelled the latest prices to the boys chalking them up on the balcony, instead of using the microphone.

Yet in the slips of paper changing hands with quick tension, the penciled notes, the ceaseless jangle of muted telephones, and, above all, the pinpointed concentration, Thatcher caught the essence of all true markets, whether they are on the waterfront at Hong Kong or the corner of John and Fulton Streets.

Without consulting the board, Thatcher knew that the price of cocoa was still falling. He did not recognize any personal acquaintances among the forty-odd men below him but, in a larger sense, he knew them all. Exhaustion hung over the Cocoa Exchange like a pall. Since nine in the morning, these men had listened, shouted, sorted rumors, and watched the sag in prices ripen into catastrophe. Like badly punished boxers, they had to keep counterpunching until the bell—relying on instinct and hope.

"Christ!" A hoarse whispered fragment from a burly man at the phone below him floated up to Thatcher. "If Amory doesn't do something today, do you know what tomorrow's going to be like?"

The restless eyes that flicked unseeingly up at Thatcher went from face to face, the questions went across the table, from messenger to trader, from telephone to telephone. But irresistibly, sooner or later, everybody turned to look at the swinging doors directly beneath Thatcher, the doors through which Amory Shaw would come.

Thatcher's hand was on the doorknob when his departure was arrested. There was a sudden hush, as compelling as an alarm bell. When Thatcher looked back, every eye was already riveted on the entrance.

Finally someone said with a hoarse assumption of jocularity: "Amory! Come to bail us out?"

The voice broke off just as Shaw came into sight directly below Thatcher. He was swaying drunkenly.

"My God!"

"Amory—"

The cries were abruptly silenced when Amory Shaw pitched forward on his face.

During the long paralysis of shock and horror Thatcher gripped the rail with painful intensity. His vantage point gave him a split-second lead over the men down below.

He was first to see the knife protruding from Amory Shaw's back.

12

"He's been knifed in the back!"

These words released frozen tongues and bodies. Questions and exclamations filled the air while stunned, incredulous men pressed forward. Thatcher lost sight of Amory Shaw in the milling confusion.

"Get back, you fools! Give him room!"

Russ Martini hurried onto the floor, thrusting people aside to clear a space around Shaw's body. Shamefacedly, his colleagues drew back, leaving him to stand guard. Looking around for help, he pointed to one of the messenger boys.

"Sam, get out to the office and tell them to find out if there's a doctor in the building," he ordered. "And have them call an ambulance."

Martini had met the emergency instinctively but, as Sam scurried away, he had second thoughts. Everybody else had stepped aside, tacitly abdicating responsibility. Martini looked down at the body and winced.

"Isn't there anybody here from Dreyer?" he asked almost desperately.

From the crowd, a voice volunteered: "I'll see if I can find someone."

It was no escape. Visibly bracing himself, Martini knelt down and studied Shaw's face.

"Is he alive, Russ?" a trader asked anxiously.

"How the hell do I know?" Martini snapped. Then, more calmly, he added: "I don't think he's breathing."

This triggered advice, argument, debate until the arrival of a newcomer.

"Good God, it's true," cried Howard Vandevanter unbelievingly. "But you can't leave him lying there. We've got to take out that knife."

He was reaching for it when Martini's hand clamped around his wrist like a vise.

"For Christ's sake, he'll hemorrhage to death if you do that. And we're not moving him either."

Vandevanter jerked his wrist free. "I don't see—" he began.

"Stand aside, please," came a brisk voice.

The doctor was escorted by Gene Orcutt, who looked as if he had been running. "Dr. Tyler here was just on his way to see his broker. Sam told me . . ."

But there was nothing Dr. Tyler could do. After a quick examination, he shook his head and rose.

"This man is dead," he said, dusting his knees automatically.

In the ensuing stillness broken only by the clangor of unanswered telephones, Orcutt sounded sick. "And the police want everybody who saw anything to stay here."

Above his head, John Thatcher sighed. If this meant anyone, it meant him.

There was no use waiting it out in solitary splendor. Thatcher made his way downstairs to the Exchange office, where he found a familiar-looking woman sobbing on Curtis Yeoman's shoulder.

"Shaw's secretary," Yeoman muttered. "She came down as soon as she heard."

She was not the only one. Murder had transformed the ground floor into a seething maelstrom. The eye of the storm was circulating around Sam, who was holding court in the narrow hallway.

"I saw the whole thing," he repeated himself excitedly. "The elevator door opened, and there was Mr. Shaw—all alone. I could tell right away something was real wrong, but I didn't know what. He didn't say anything. He just staggered past me, toward the floor. He was halfway there before I saw the knife in his back. Christ, it was awful."

"They killed him," moaned the woman in Yeoman's arms. "They murdered Mr. Shaw."

"For God's sake," Howard Vandevanter protested as he appeared. "I know this is terrible, Mrs. Macomber, but try to get hold of yourself. The police will be here any minute and hysterical accusations won't help."

"Well, she's right, isn't she?" Yeoman asked nastily.

Vandevanter produced a handkerchief and wearily mopped his brow. "I suppose so. I couldn't believe it when they told me. I'd just come down from Glasscock's office . . ."

Yeoman's head jerked back. "That's funny. I didn't see you there, and God knows I was looking for you."

"We must have just missed each other," Vandevanter wanted to drop the subject.

"I was looking for you too," said Gene Orcutt dully. "That's why I came downstairs . . ."

Mrs. Macomber had been following her own line of thought. Unerringly she said what nobody wanted to hear.

"Oh, poor Mr. Frohlich," she wailed. "First him—now, Mr. Shaw."

Yeoman cast her a look of venomous dislike, then deliberately turned to Thatcher. "Can't somebody do something about this mob?" he complained. "Everybody in the building seems to be shoving their way down here."

"Well, what the hell do you expect?"

Thatcher swung around to find Leo Gilligan, standing apart, smoking a cigar.

"Hello, Gilligan," he said. "I didn't notice you."

"I came down to see what was happening to September delivery," said Gilligan with a wry smile. "And I found—this!"

Before Thatcher could comment, there was a sudden increase of activity outside. From Fulton Street, a phalanx of policemen began hurrying in to be met by a crowd exiting from the floor.

"Great," said Gilligan bitterly. "Trading is closed for the day." He gave a cracked laugh. "If trading is what you call it."

Two hours later he was downing a glass. "I needed that," he said, signaling the waiter for another round.

"Come on, Leo," said Charlie Trinkam comfortably. "What are you worrying about? I'll back up your alibi."

Gilligan was not smiling. "You worry about alibis. I've got my hands full, worrying about going broke."

Curious, Thatcher asked: "How is Charlie your alibi?"

When the police had finally released their unruly band of witnesses, Thatcher had been taken aback to find Gilligan at his elbow. He was meeting Trinkam in a bar around the corner, Gilligan explained. Would Thatcher care to join them?

Lighting a fresh cigar, Gilligan now amplified: "As nearly as I can tell, I was on the telephone with Charlie here, when Amory got it."

Unlike Charlie, he was not treating that phone call lightly. Thatcher wondered how much this alibi was worth. Apparently there was several minutes' leeway as to when Amory Shaw had been stabbed.

"Well, if you were on the phone in an office," Thatcher reasoned, "presumably you've got other witnesses—"

But this was a misstep.

"Call from an office?" Gilligan scoffed. "Do I want any of those cutthroats to know I'm calling my banker, trying to raise cash? Hell, I was in a pay phone, outside. You see, I've studied Shaw. He doesn't make moves at the end of the day. I figured he was going to hold off until first thing tomorrow morning. That's why I wanted to be ready . . ."

Thatcher was willing to let Gilligan lead the conversation away from murder to cocoa futures, although he doubted that the police had been so accommodating.

Whether or not Charlie could be called an adequate alibi was an open question. He was prepared to be helpful along different lines.

"Anyway, Leo, Shaw was going to scoop the pool—and now there's no Shaw. That proves you had a lot to gain by keeping him alive."

Gilligan did not like this either. "The police aren't thinking about me," he said authoritatively. "They've got plenty to keep them busy—with Dreyer."

Nobody could contradict him. "Two murders in two weeks," Charlie marveled aloud. "I suppose the police have made the connection."

"Give them credit for some sense," Thatcher told him. "They barely finished questioning people in that building about Frohlich, when they were called in for Shaw."

"It would make anybody think twice," Charlie agreed. "I suppose your pals at Dreyer weren't lucky enough to all be sitting around the same conference table at the critical moment."

Gilligan took the remark at face value. "They don't have conferences at Dreyer here, unless Amory Shaw is in the chair."

It was going to be a long time, Thatcher reflected, before the shadow of Amory Shaw faded. "For your information, Charlie, everyone involved was alone and in motion at the time of the murder. The police even had trouble tracking Shaw. He was in his own office, he stopped by Martini & Mears, he went downstairs to Frohlich's old office. And he was on and off the floor itself. The police assume he was attacked in the elevator, or just as he was getting into it."

Charlie ironed out details to his own satisfaction. "And it would only take a second. You walk up to Shaw, plunge the knife in, then skedaddle." He accompanied this recital with exuberant gestures. "By all odds, Shaw should have been dead when the elevator doors opened downstairs."

"Yes," Thatcher nodded. "His staggering onto the floor was a macabre touch that doesn't alter things at all."

"It's a shame he didn't use his energy to whisper the murderer's name to somebody."

"The medical theory is there was nothing rational about Shaw's last movements—just a spasmodic attempt to find help."

It was always a mistake to hurl medical theories at Charlie. "Like those galvanic kicks from the frog, huh?" he asked.

Gilligan shuddered. "Listen, I've got to get back," he said, rising. "You're giving me a call later, Charlie? I don't know what the hell's going to happen tomorrow, but I still want to be ready . . ."

Charlie sped him on his way with reassurance, then studied the table top soberly.

"Leo's worried," he concluded. "The way things are going in cocoa, he'd be nuts if he wasn't. But I sure as hell hope that one of our big customers isn't going to turn out to be Jack the Ripper."

Thatcher could not dismiss the possibility out of hand. "The attack could have taken place on any floor. Nobody noticed the elevator indicator. So, everyone is still in the running."

Charlie digested this. Then: "What about Vandevanter wanting to pull the knife out? Maybe he was scared to find Shaw still alive, and wanted to finish the job."

"That's one interpretation," Thatcher agreed. "You could also say that Vandevanter was in shock. Or that he meant it for the best. The trouble is that there are too many possibilities. Vandevanter managed to shake his flunkies and was roaming around, hunting for Shaw. Yeoman was on his trail. Orcutt seems to have been looking for either of them—"

"I'm surprised they didn't all run into each other in the men's room," said Charlie.

"Orcutt claims to have checked them all—looking for Shaw." When Charlie laughed, he added: "Of course, you can cast a wider net, too. Take Martini, for instance. He went outside to grab a bite, and there's no corroboration about when he got back."

"Boy," said Charlie admiringly, "that's some bunch you're mixed up with, John. I can hardly wait for the next installment from Dreyer."

He did not have to wait long. As they were settling the bill, the television set in the corner erupted into choral chanting: *D-R-E-Y-E-R spells Dreyer*.

"That's one hell of a way to announce a murder," said Charlie thoughtfully.

It was not, as Thatcher had momentarily feared, the news.

"Tonight," said an unctuous voice, "we are presenting Dreyer's Living Theater, to celebrate the introduction of Dreyer's Old Glory. Yes, America's first family of fine chocolate brings you the ultimate satisfaction in a candy bar. Made with only natural ingredients, Old Glory blends the creamy satisfaction of milk chocolate from an old Swiss recipe with the tart refreshment of pure bittersweet. For almost a century, Americans on the go have turned to Dreyer for . . ."

The screen showed a rural couple in turn-of-the-century attire. The husband, resting from the plow, munched a candy bar. Instantly fatigue vanished, and he bounded back to Old Dobbin. Much the same transpired with his wife at her back porch mangle.

"Good Lord," said Thatcher. "Kanelos' advertising campaign!"

The drama moved to current times. This couple, in blue jeans, were swinging through a landscape rich in meadow flowers. Hand in hand, they brandished Old Glory bars at each other.

"Like their grandparents before them," said the announcer, "they settle for nothing but the best."

The young couple paused to embrace. A balmy breeze played over their golden locks while the sound track broke into romantic strains. The young man drew back, looked soulfully at his companion, then addressed himself to a chocolate bar.

"When you need that extra ounce of quick energy,"

106

said the voice solemnly, "reach for a Dreyer's Old Glory."

Charlie didn't believe what he was hearing. "Are they trying to tell me he can't get it up without some candy?"

"Ssh!" begged the bar, glued to the screen.

But Dreyer's was a family product. The young lovers faded slowly from view.

"Say," somebody was reminded, "didn't they have another murder over at Dreyer today?"

"Well, there's a new twist for you," Charlie remarked. "I wonder how much it's costing Dreyer to go on network TV and remind us all that they specialize in murder, as well as chocolate."

13

In the midst of life, so the scripture runs, there is death. This sober truth provides its own measure of comfort at even the most tragic bereavement. The reverse, equally true, always causes more trouble. At the Cocoa Exchange on Friday morning, they were grappling with the fact that life must continue even after death.

"All right, all right!" Wayne Glasscock exploded. "Amory Shaw got murdered next door. With the police crawling all over the place, I'm not likely to forget it, am I? But what do you want me to do? Close the goddam Exchange?"

"Take it easy, Wayne," urged his companion. But a trader who had just returned to their table after a quick reconnaissance was more hard-nosed.

"Might not be a bad idea," he said.

Today's midmorning kaffee klatsch in the Exchange's paneled lunchroom was short on the usual banter about hockey teams, suburban crime, and new secretaries. Even so, Russ Martini, slumped in the corner chair, raised his head to see if Severinson was joking.

"I wish to God I could," said Glasscock fervently.

Severinson, the floor man from Clayton Anderson, laughed hollowly. "Boy, talk about a mark of respect. That would be something, wouldn't it? Closing the Cocoa Exchange in memory of Amory Shaw!"

This bit too close to the bone. What had happened to Amory Shaw was overshadowed by what was happening next door, on the floor. It was not far short of disaster.

"I'd better get back and spell Jim," Martini said with genuine reluctance. Today, going onto the floor was like climbing onto an anvil. The hammer of crumbling prices was inexorable.

"I wonder what Dreyer is going to do now?" Severinson asked the glum silence.

"Sooner or later, they've got to buy—"

For once Severinson was not reverting to that all-important theme, as he hastened to explain: "No, I meant who is Dreyer going to replace Amory with?"

Like the first fugitive breath of cool air after a heat wave, this relief was revivifying.

"Good God!" Wayne Glasscock straightened in his chair. "Do you know that in all those hours last night with the police in and out—I never thought of that. And then this morning—"

By common consent, the subject of what happened in the first two hours of trading was dropped.

"Orcutt?" said Severinson tentatively.

His suggestion evoked derisive snorts, a shrug from Glasscock, and an unfortunate observation from the swinger in the lavender double-knit.

"They wouldn't touch Orcutt," he contributed, adding: "Besides, Orcutt's still in trouble with the police, isn't he, Russ?"

Clambering unwillingly to his feet, Martini suppressed a curse. Thanks to a few minutes yesterday in the limelight with Amory Shaw's body, he was now the local expert on the murder and the murder investigation. Holding on to his patience, he answered: "I understand they gave him a pretty good going over. Apparently he was in and out of a lot of offices, so that he doesn't have an alibi—"

Glasscock forgot about tact. "That isn't enough to explain why the police are concentrating on him," he said didactically. "If one thing came through yesterday, it was that nobody has an alibi. Vandevanter was in and out of my office—"

He broke off when Martini's grimace reminded him that among those without an alibi was Martini himself.

"So," said Martini as if there had been no interruption, "they've started casting around for motives."

"That lets all of us out," said Severinson devoutly. "If there's one thing everybody on the Cocoa Exchange would like, it's Amory Shaw—alive and buying."

Martini ignored this too. "Orcutt has been doing a little trading on his own. The cops put that together with the fact that Dick Frohlich was trading for himself—"

Several voices made it a ragged chorus. "But everybody does."

"Don't tell me," said Martini. "Tell the cops. Anyway, that's the story on why the police were giving Orcutt such a hard time. Unless there's something else I don't know about."

"What if Dreyer does promote him?" Severinson reverted to his original theme. "Say, that could be a motive, couldn't it?"

"You know what, Carl," said Martini with reasonably good nature. "When you sound off like that, you make going back onto the floor a pleasure."

Nobody was in any danger of taking these words at face value.

* * *

Concerning death as well as life, women are tougher than men, as Helen Nagle was demonstrating.

"If you don't call him, I will," she said, underscoring the ultimatum by folding her arms virago-fashion.

Fred cast around for support. A passing dolly, loaded to the gills with White Owls destined for Baltimore, gave none. He fell back on the logic that had been so fruitless during the preceding half-hour.

"Look, Helen, we went over it all last night," he said doggedly. "In the first place, I don't think there's anything I can do. And you remember how uptight Vandevanter was in Princeton. Now they've had two murders—"

"Exactly," said Helen distinctly. "I don't care if they've got a hundred murders at Dreyer. If you don't get on the phone to tell Vandevanter to call off this advertising campaign, I will. And don't tell me it's none of our business—" she gestured toward the utility shelving of Arrow Jobbers, Inc., piled high with carton after carton labeled *Old Glory,* took a deep breath, and continued—*"and,* so long as we're splitting the local promo costs, we've got plenty to say! Either you say it, or I do."

"Now, Helen—"

"Don't *Now Helen* me!" she shouted unfairly, since despite his protest Fred was heading for the telephone. For once, Helen was too heated to be generous in triumph. "Doesn't Dreyer have *any* sense at all?"

Last night had been bad enough. The six-thirty news barely summarized the latest Middle-East incident before the first commercial. A carefree band of beautiful young people frolicked in smog-free sunshine on a pristine beach. Leapfrogging each other, turning cartwheels, they simultaneously flourished their bars and yodeled: *For a Glorious Taste, Taste Dreyer's Old Glory.* Immediately thereafter, CBS, NBC, and ABC informed the nation that Amory Shaw, a vice-president of the Dreyer Chocolate Company, had been brutally murdered on the floor of the New York Cocoa Exchange.

By eleven o'clock, the hot medium had not only caught up with Bridges, Gray & Kanelos, it had overtaken them.

First the public saw happy Princeton families, trekking into the Corner Newspaper Store to buy Dreyer's delicious Old Glory. The cutaway was to a stretcher being carted out of the Cocoa Exchange.

When they retired Thursday night, Fred and Helen Nagle were in their usual harmony. The murder of Amory Shaw was admittedly a terrible thing. But they had not known him, and the tragedy soon became commingled with uneasy speculations about the Dreyer Chocolate Company.

The parting of their ways came Friday morning, with the *Today Show*. Bridges, Gray & Kanelos had surpassed itself. Old Glory, they said, came from the patroon country of upstate New York. Its goodness came to fruition in the rich meadows and lush grasses of the Mohawk Valley. The original settlers had brought with them the Old World secrets of their milk chocolate. This commercial featured rosy-cheeked lasses in Dutch national costume, pausing in a country dance with their swains to pick up wooden buckets and swish to the side of gently chomping cattle. With a song on their lips, they set to work, milking the noble beasts. It was bucolic, it was peaceful, it was uplifting. It was also, as Fred did point out, totally unlike modern dairy practices anywhere—including the Netherlands.

However, what the scene lacked in accuracy, it made up in relevance to the opening news item.

"Police today revealed that Amory Shaw is the second Dreyer executive to be killed within the last two weeks. On September twelfth in Dreyer, New York, Richard Frohlich was found murdered. Frohlich worked in the New York City offices of Dreyer, close to Amory Shaw, yesterday's victim. We switch you now to Dreyer . . ."

This time there were no dirndls—only the chief of police explaining how closely Dreyer and New York officials were cooperating. There followed shots of a motel, an industrial compound, and, irony of ironies, the dairies of the Dreyer Chocolate Company, complete with milking machines, conveyer belts, and union representatives.

"You know, Fred," said Helen, switching off the portable TV, "if they had any brains at Dreyer, they'd postpone the advertising push until these murders aren't such hot news."

Fred, a peaceable man, spoke about commitments, contracts and time slots, then departed for the Arrow Jobbers warehouse. This left Helen to her thoughts—and morning TV.

Dreyer's Kiddy Magic Show ("Send us two Old Glory wrappers and we'll send you a Dreyer Wonder Wand!") led to several station break spots: "Salute Old Glory!" "Old Glory packs a chocolaty punch!" This, in turn, was followed by the noon news, where a sex kitten impersonating Hamlet's mother intoned the latest headlines: ". . . still investigating the second murder. Employees in New York and Dreyer are being questioned. Meanwhile, in Washington, aides to the president . . ."

This sent Helen hightailing out to New Jersey for one of her rare descents on Arrow Jobbers.

"And don't let him tell you that any publicity is good publicity," she said, settling on the corner of Fred's desk.

"All right, all right," he grumbled, eying the phone warily.

"Go on!"

You can lead a horse to water; you may be able to make him drink; you sure as hell cannot expect the horse to thank you.

"I was just trying to figure out where Vandevanter might be," Fred stalled. "We know he was in the city yesterday. But maybe he went back to Dreyer . . ."

It did not matter. The metallic voices in both New York and Dreyer had one programmed response. Mr. Vandevanter was not available. If Mr. Nagle cared to leave a message . . .

Shamefacedly trying to mask his relief, Fred was ready

to join Helen in denouncing this runaround when she jolted him by saying: "Well, then! Call Kanelos!"

For a split second, he goggled at her. Then, Fred Nagle came down heavily for being a man, not a mouse. "The hell I will!"

Before either of them could see where this would lead, the phone jangled into life. Fred fell on it gratefully. "Nagle . . . yes, George . . . What? Wait a minute until I get a pencil . . . now, that's two dozen gross? . . . Sure . . . on the morning truck . . . fine . . . fine . . ."

He replaced the receiver, jotted a few notes, then said: "How do you like that? George Savard. He wants two dozen gross of Old Glory. Apparently people have been asking for it all morning . . ."

This brought Helen back to earth with a thump. Decisively, she changed course. "Then the last person you want to talk to is Ted Kanelos."

"*Or* Howard Vandevanter," said Fred, pressing his advantage. "Say what you will, Old Glory is a lot more important to the Dreyer Chocolate Company than Amory Shaw ever was."

Somehow or other it was a chilling thought, even at Arrow Jobbers.

Friday was a long, hard day at the Cocoa Exchange and at Arrow Jobbers. They were feeling the pressure in the stark bastion of new police headquarters, too. Official spokesmen, alerted by the mayor's office and a lot of high-priced lawyers, had scheduled a progress report to press, radio, and TV at three o'clock.

"That's a laugh," said Captain Jacobsen, summing up the mood of his colleagues.

Hours of digging were paying off with a tantalizing hodgepodge of information, but nobody was ready to call this progress yet. By now, Detective Al Marziello had the support of a massive scientific establishment as he restated the fundamental problem.

"Somebody sticks an ordinary knife in Shaw's back. Somehow or other—and Doc Lolich says it happens more often than you think—Shaw doesn't drop dead. He gets down to the lobby, heads for the floor—"

"And no one except that kid, Sam, notices a thing," Jacobsen interjected. "Until Shaw collapses."

"And Sam," Marziello said phlegmatically, "is none too bright. He trails along with his mouth open . . ."

A collective sigh went around the table. They all knew what came next.

"Before this, we've got people saying Shaw stopped by the president's office, that broker's, and even Frohlich's office. But nobody is exactly sure about the times. In other words, it was a perfectly normal day."

"Except that everybody was looking for him," Jacobsen said. "Granted, the Cocoa Exchange is an easy place to miss connections in . . ."

"Or *claim* that you've missed connections," Marziello corrected.

Detective Udall cleared his throat. "And it wasn't a really normal day," he said with the quiet confidence of an expert in financial manipulation. "The cocoa market was in shambles. Everybody over there was down on their knees, praying for Amory Shaw to start buying."

Marziello had already scowled his way through Udall's explanation of Amory Shaw's role in cocoa. Now, almost humbly, he said: "It's all too deep for me. But Dennis, could somebody have knocked Shaw off to keep him from buying? People make money that way, too, don't they?"

Udall looked tired. "It's a possibility," he said. "In which case, we're never going to find out who killed Shaw. Anybody could have walked in off the street, slipped the knife in, then walked right out again. But, in the meantime, we're checking the trading of the people most closely involved . . ."

"Orcutt?" Marziello asked quickly.

"Him, as well as others," said Udall. "But, none of them stands to make a killing."

Jacobsen had a different approach. "Shaw and Frohlich," he said ponderously. "And throw in *Mr.* Howard

114

Vandevanter and *Governor* Curtis Yeoman—and what've you got?"

Despite the sarcastic honorifics, they all knew. "You've got the Dreyer Chocolate Company—no matter what anybody says, including our pal up in Dreyer."

Supercareful responses by Vandevanter and Yeoman were only what the New York Police Department expected. But Captain Huggins of the Dreyer force was a continuing irritant. By telephone and teletype that cooperation vaunted on national television had been forthcoming.

"But he's too damned respectful about the Dreyer Chocolate Company!" Jacobsen complained.

"He's not the only one," said Detective Udall. "They're all playing it pretty cozy at the Exchange, too. Nobody wants to say too much. I've picked up a couple of rumors about a big fight between Amory Shaw and Vandevanter."

"Like the fight between Frohlich and Orcutt," said Marziello. "Maybe the best move is to get back to Vandevanter—"

Unceremoniously, Jacobsen dismissed this. "We'll get back to him, but Vandevanter's not giving anything away. He says there were no company problems—just the ordinary disagreements you find where executives have different jurisdictions. Everybody deferred to Amory Shaw when it came to cocoa futures . . ."

"I wonder what they'll do now," murmured Udall when Jacobsen trailed off in disgust.

"Whatever it is, we'll have to wait and see," said Jacobsen. "Because all we'll get out of Mr. Howard Vandevanter is a lot of bullshit."

The outlook for this afternoon's progress report, and any subsequent ones, was bleak.

Then, Udall had an idea.

"Talking to Vandevanter again will probably be a waste of time—"

"That goes for that gas bag Yeoman, too," Marziello added.

"—but I know someone we let off pretty lightly yesterday."

John Putnam Thatcher should have seen this one coming.

14

Thatcher had not expected Friday to be any picnic. When Krakatau exploded, skies around the globe darkened with matter belched from the bowels of the earth. With the murder of Amory Shaw and bedlam in the cocoa market—not to speak of Union Funding—only a fool would have looked forward to sunshine and light on Wall Street.

What rained down on his defenseless head, however, was unexpected.

"Thank God, it's Friday," said Tom Robichaux. A complete and refreshing lack of originality had been one of his enduring characteristics since their student days in Harvard Yard.

"It's been quite a week," Thatcher agreed, reflecting that he too was beginning to repeat himself. Still, stock replies were the safest, whether it came to Union Funding or Amory Shaw.

"I've always thanked God that Robichaux & Devane doesn't have anything to do with commodities," said the senior partner with his own idiosyncratic perspective. "Bad as things are, we're not sticking knives in people's backs."

"Not yet," said Thatcher uncompromisingly. Things were not simply bad over at Tom's shop; they were terrible. Robichaux & Devane was up to its neck in litigation with all comers, including two Swiss banks and the Dartmouth Endowment Fund, concerning delivery of (and payment for) Union Funding common.

Robichaux did not scout the suggestion. Instead, following a train of thought that eluded Thatcher, he said: "Jennifer and I are getting a divorce."

"Good God," said Thatcher, for once rising to the occasion.

"I knew you'd be surprised to hear it," said Tom, tucking into Luchow's sauerbraten with lugubrious satisfaction.

The law of diminishing returns made this highly unlikely, although Tom's latest matrimonial debacle was not totally without interest.

". . . since she isn't Jewish, I began wondering why Jennifer kept running back and forth to Israel. Of course, I know travel is broadening. Did you know that *sabra* has something to do with pears . . . ?"

Long ago, Thatcher had suspended judgment on how deeply Robichaux felt these nonstop conjugal dislocations of his. It was unworthy to wonder if Jennifer and her tour leader—they seemed to have taken long, long hikes in the Negev—did not make a nice change from Union Funding.

". . . reasonable settlement," Tom was saying virtuously. Then his face darkened. "But Jennifer's dug up some smart lawyer . . ."

While he relieved pent-up emotion with a frontal assault on the mashed potatoes, Thatcher remained discreetly silent. *Reasonable settlements* and *smart lawyers* boded ill for Tom Robichaux in connection with either Jennifer or Union Funding.

"Well, I suppose things could be worse." Tom's philosophic conclusion sprang from a substantial family fortune, rather than inner grace. "Take whatsisname!"

He was the only one Thatcher was destined to meet that Friday in a position to forget Amory Shaw's name.

Certainly Detective Dennis Udall was not.

Thatcher was making progress through yet another op-

117

timistic study of oil shale when Miss Corsa, after purely nominal warning, ushered the policeman in.

"First I want to say that we appreciate any cooperation you can give us," Udall began earnestly.

"I believe I told the detectives everything I had done or seen at the Cocoa Exchange," Thatcher replied. "But anything further I can do to help . . . Won't you sit down?"

Udall did so and Miss Corsa decorously withdrew. The cooperation had been all hers. Thatcher's request for an uninterrupted afternoon would have been good against most suppliants, including the president of the Sloan Guaranty Trust. But with the New York Police Department, Miss Corsa did not even stop to think. Thatcher himself believed that citizens should aid law enforcement authorities, but he did not go to Miss Corsa's fanatic extremes. Any day now she was going to turn up in one of those posses that prey upon would-be muggers.

Udall, it developed, did not want to review Thatcher's exhaustive account of the Old Glory press conference, or Amory Shaw's collapse on the floor.

"Everything you told us jibes with what other witnesses have said," he observed while Thatcher wracked his brain for details he might have overlooked. "What I want to talk to you about, Mr. Thatcher, is the situation at the Dreyer Chocolate Company."

Thatcher was unpleasantly jolted, although he hoped it did not show. He fully recognized the police had a legitimate interest in the Dreyer Chocolate Company. On the other hand, the last few weeks had made him privy to some, if not all, of Dreyer's secrets. It was a fine line, and there was only one way to handle it.

"My personal acquaintance with the Dreyer Chocolate Company is of relatively short duration," he said forcefully. "Dating from my appointment to the Leonard Dreyer Trust . . ."

"That would be the beginning of September?"

Udall inserted this casually but Thatcher took note. He would have liked to say that his contacts with Dreyer's front office had been limited. But two of those limited contacts, after all, had involved murder. The prudent thing to do was sit tight, and let Udall lead the way.

Udall showed himself to be reasonable as well as competent. There were no questions about the interplay of personalities at Dreyer—at least not directly. Instead, he zeroed in on areas where Thatcher could not plead ignorance.

"I understand," he said with unconvincing hesitation, "that you were present during a confrontation between Amory Shaw and Howard Vandevanter, in the office of the president of the Cocoa Exchange."

"There was quite a crowd of us," Thatcher replied with a grin, certain that Udall had already ticked them off. It did not require much reflection to see why Udall wanted his version. Glasscock, Russ Martini, and, above all, Howard Vandevanter had solid reasons to downplay the scene.

Even Curtis Yeoman was probably guarding his tongue.

"Vandevanter and Shaw differed about Dreyer employees' trading in cocoa futures on their own, didn't they?" asked Udall, carefully not mentioning the employee who sprang to mind.

With similar care, Thatcher obliged with a comprehensive, but arid, description of the dispute which had culminated in Glasscock's office. Udall, he had a shrewd notion, knew all he needed to know about the intricacies of futures trading and the customs of the cocoa trade. If not, there were plenty of people over at John Street better qualified than Thatcher to clue him in.

To his credit, Udall showed no disappointment when the thin end of his wedge produced neither vivid characterization nor editorial comment.

Instead, he simply remarked: "Feelings can run high over that sort of thing."

Thatcher contemplated asking if the police thought Amory Shaw's murder was a crime of passion, but decided that Udall was too serious-minded.

"Vandevanter and Shaw were strongly defending their respective positions—and making no bones about it. But, in all fairness, I should add that Martini, the broker, as well as Glasscock, were not backward about expressing themselves. After all, large sums of money were involved, as well as established usage."

But he was not getting off that easily.

"Were any accusations made?" Udall asked. "Did Vandevanter think Shaw, for example, was using Dreyer to feather his own nest?"

"Specifically, and more than once, he repeated that he was not suggesting any impropriety by Shaw," said Thatcher, relying on the literal truth to speak for itself.

Udall tried a different tack. "Did you get the impression that this did not really concern private trading? That it was just part of a power struggle between Shaw and Vandevanter?"

Thatcher was firm. "I got the impression that two strong-willed men were meeting head-on over an important issue."

"And whose side was Governor Yeoman on?" asked Udall quietly.

Thatcher was not temporizing when he replied: "Governor Yeoman took almost no part in the discussion in Glasscock's office. To be honest I was surprised by his lack of participation."

At the end of another twenty minutes, Udall was in full possession of the facts at Thatcher's disposition. His bland expression gave no hint as to his interpretation of them. Nevertheless Thatcher thought he could hazard a guess.

All he said when he finally took his departure was: "Thank you again, Mr. Thatcher. This has been very helpful."

Thatcher had been too scrupulously precise to have said anything to regret. Even so, the interlude reinforced his strong inclination to keep distance between himself and the tortuous affairs of Dreyer Chocolate.

This resolution stood for the remainder of the afternoon at the Sloan. Miss Corsa, although unrepentant about capitulating to the police, reestablished an effective defense perimeter. This left Thatcher at least theoretically free to think long and hard about oil shale.

It was in his own apartment that evening that the axe fell.

15

"Is that you, Thatcher?"

The whisper on the phone sounded conspiratorial.

Thatcher's immediate reaction was irritation, pure and simple. This was his telephone. This was his apartment. Who else was it likely to be? But, since he thought he recognized his caller, he said only: "What can I do for you, Vandevanter?"

As he spoke he was assailed by misgivings. Possibly Howard Vandevanter had caught wind of Detective Udall's research into Dreyer's latest infighting. If so, Thatcher could be in for a long, tedious harangue.

But relief came gusting over the line, not indignation or self-pity. "Thank God! I was afraid I might not be able to catch you at such short notice. Thatcher, something very important has come up. That's why I'm going to ask you for a favor . . ."

Instinctively, Thatcher braced himself for the worst.

Vandevanter's next words came as an anticlimax. ". . . asking a lot, I know. But can you spare me an hour of your time tonight?"

John Thatcher was, if anything, overinclined to invent previous engagements on the spur of the moment. But Vandevanter's urgency piqued his curiosity and slowed him down.

Vandevanter seized the opportunity to plead his case. ". . . it could make or break Dreyer!"

Under the circumstances, Thatcher could scarcely refuse.

"I'd be glad to be of assistance—" he began.

"Good, good!" Vandevanter broke in. "Now we've got to keep news of this from getting around! What I want you to do is this . . ."

Ten minutes later Thatcher was plodding through the sodden misery of a late September downpour in New York. The unforgiving wind turned raindrops into missiles, rattling window panes, assaulting umbrellas, drowning clogged sewers.

The few cruising taxis were not worth the fight. Thatcher always found walking conducive to thought and utilized this interval to canvass possibilities. None of them explained to his satisfaction why Howard Vandevanter needed him at the New York Hilton.

"Nobody will notice you in the lobby. It's always jammed," Vandevanter had explained. "You come right up to my suite on the seventeenth floor. I moved in here today purposely to have a place where we could meet without causing comment . . ."

If anything, this raised more questions than it answered. The Dreyer Chocolate Company had many offices in New York, as well as permanent quarters for traveling executives at the Waldorf.

Why this last-minute flight to the Hilton?

Thatcher was still theorizing when he hurried across Sixth Avenue, directly into the path of two men barreling northward.

"John!" Charlie Trinkam was never dampened by mere weather. "This is one hell of a night to be taking a constitutional."

Leo Gilligan confined himself to a brief: "Evening, Thatcher!"

"I'll join you," said Thatcher, catching a glimmer of

light. "I take it that you two are on your way to the Hilton."

This earned him a sharp look from Charlie, but Gilligan seemed to accept Thatcher's presence as perfectly natural.

"I hope Vandevanter isn't trying to pull some sort of fast one," he said when they stood dripping in the Hilton lobby. He looked around with discontent: men with attaché cases lined up at the desk, family parties celebrating wedding anniversaries, conventioneers hailing conventioneers. "Why have us all sneaking around in the middle of the night? Why meetings in hotel rooms? I don't know what Vandevanter thinks he's up to—but it'd better be good. After the day we put in down at the Exchange—"

"How bad was it, Leo?" Charlie asked him.

"Hell," he replied tersely. "A couple more like it—"

He finished the sentence by drawing a stubby hand across his throat.

Thatcher had no reason to doubt Leo Gilligan's reading. He already knew that cocoa prices were still tumbling—and that most speculators, like most gamblers, count on the upside.

But was it likely that Gilligan had braved the elements tonight with no inkling of what Howard Vandevanter wanted?

Charlie could sometimes read Thatcher's mind. "Leo says Vandevanter has a proposition for him. He decided that—all things considered—he wanted a witness."

Given the implications, Thatcher remained carefully expressionless.

"I think that may be my function as well."

It would not be the first time that the Sloan Guaranty Trust fielded a team of official observers. Thatcher was just deciding that he could make a fair guess at the truce terms, when the door to 1701 was flung open.

"Come in!" Vandevanter was more anxious than cordial.

Only when they had filed in did he notice Charlie.

"What are you . . . oh, I suppose Mr. Gilligan asked

you . . . well, of course that's fine . . . as a matter of fact, I invited Thatcher . . ."

Sardonically, Gilligan interrupted: "Is there someplace we can hang up our coats?"

Vandevanter had neglected to draw the drapes across the large, rain-streaked window. Remains of a dinner awaited room service. An open door off the characterless sitting room yielded glimpses of a rumpled bed.

All in all, thought Thatcher as Vandevanter awkwardly relieved him of his soaked raincoat, not an auspicious beginning.

"Can I offer anybody a drink?" asked Vandevanter. "No? Well, then . . ."

Without looking, Thatcher knew what Charlie and Leo Gilligan were thinking. Starting negotiations, no matter what they are about, by displaying tension and discomfort is a serious mistake. Howard Vandevanter would have been much more effective behind a Dreyer desk, in a Dreyer office.

By contrast, Gilligan settled in the corner of the sofa and unwrapped his cigar with conspicuous ease.

"What was it you wanted to talk to me about, Vandevanter?" he asked.

Vandevanter was either deaf to the bored tone, or determined to ignore it.

"You know, of course, that Dreyer has to replace Amory Shaw as rapidly as possible," he began. "The final choice will take some time. The board and I have discussed it, and we decided to approach you, Mr. Gilligan. Would you be willing to take charge of our cocoa trading—on a pro-tem basis?"

Gilligan did not even pretend to be surprised. "Spell it out for me," he directed.

Vandevanter glanced at a note, then launched on a prepared text about financial arrangements. While he outlined handsome salary terms, Gilligan sat with narrowed eyes. But when he wound up, there was no immediate response. Finally, Gilligan said:

"I'm willing to think about your offer. But first, we'd

better get some things out in the open." Pointedly he glanced toward Thatcher and Charlie as if reminding Vandevanter of their presence. "Why me? Why not someone from Dreyer? Someone in your Purchasing Division—or even Gene Orcutt. Have you considered promoting him?"

Vandevanter had anticipated this, and was ready with fluent evasion. "We have reviewed the total situation of Dreyer in New York. There is nobody suitable to do Amory Shaw's job. As for Orcutt, it appears that Amory did not use him as an assistant in any meaningful sense of the word. He was not in Amory's confidence, nor does he have adequate experience—"

"Has he asked for the job?" Gilligan demanded baldly.

Looking uncomfortable, Vandevanter nodded. "Yes, he spoke to me about it this afternoon. But I made it perfectly clear to him that it was not possible. We have agreed to continue him in his present capacity."

Gilligan thought about this, then said flatly: "That's not a very good idea."

Before Vandevanter could defend himself, Gilligan methodically began putting other cards on the table: "Now, there's something else we'd better talk over. If I go to work for Dreyer, I want the same free hand that Amory Shaw had. I'll make the decisions, about when to buy and sell. The way the market is going, whoever takes over is going to be doing some heavy trading in the next few weeks."

Vandevanter accepted this condition as soon as it was out of Gilligan's mouth. "Yes," he said quickly. "We understand that completely. Dreyer has to have an experienced man in charge—" He broke off, then lamely tried to avoid conceding too much. "Naturally, we expect to maintain close contact with you about your operations—just as we did with Amory. Daily consultations would be necessary . . ."

Thatcher expected Gilligan to tear into this. But Amory

Shaw was dead and gone. Gilligan made no comment on the past reporting between New York and Dreyer, except for a contemptuous: "Sure." Then he went on to something more important. "Now, let's get it all straight about my trading on my own account."

"It is not," said Vandevanter emphatically, "a practice that Dreyer encourages."

With Detective Udall fresh in his mind's eye, Thatcher was hard put to keep from commenting. Gilligan was more brutal.

"Uh huh," he said almost conversationally. "I hear you raised hell with Amory about it."

"We discussed—"

"You tried getting reports from brokers, you tried to get the Exchange to monitor insider trading." Gilligan was studying a lengthening cigar ash as he sunk these accurate shafts.

"We had some exploratory discussions," Vandevanter insisted. "They were highly confidential—"

"Confidential, my foot! There are plenty of secrets down at the Exchange—but not that kind of crap. Everybody knows a lot more about what Dreyer people are doing—or trying to do—than you think, Mr. Vandevanter. And that includes the police."

This plain talk silenced Howard Vandevanter.

Gilligan remained in command: "Charlie here can tell you that my dealings in cocoa aren't chicken feed. If I accept your offer, I'd have to cut back a little—that's only reasonable. But I am not prepared to give up my own activity in cocoa—and I want that clearly understood by you and everybody else."

While Vandevanter struggled between what he wanted and what he needed, Gilligan mercilessly laid it on the line: "I could milk Dreyer by using my position to get in fast and make a killing for myself. Hell, I could even cost you money if I started playing fast and loose with how I bought and sold for Dreyer."

For many reasons Thatcher wished Vandevanter could

counter with an equally candid statement. When he did not, Gilligan continued:

"But if that worries you, then you're making a mistake even talking to me. Either you trust me, or you don't. And right now, I think you've got to trust me. Unless you get somebody who knows what he's doing in Shaw's office pretty damned fast, Dreyer is going to be in worse difficulties than it already is."

Too late, Vandevanter pulled himself together. His remarks about confidence and reliance left much to be desired. Gilligan barely heard him out before he struck again with a further question.

"By the way, you said you talked this over with your board? Does that include Governor Yeoman?"

"Why, yes," said Vandevanter, bewildered. For the first time, Thatcher sympathized with him. This was one he had not seen coming, either.

"And he goes along with your offering me the job?" Gilligan persisted.

"Certainly he does," said Vandevanter positively. "As I recall, he said that he would accept any decision about a temporary replacement that I made. But why do you ask?"

Leo Gilligan was not afraid to speak his mind. "Because Governor Yeoman was around when Amory Shaw got murdered. From what I hear, he's been around a lot. Before I do anything I regret, I want to know the lay of the land."

While Vandevanter stared, he strolled over to look out on New York's rain-blurred night lights. Then, rocking back on his heels, he summed up: "I'm ready to leave it at that. I'll consider the offer, Vandevanter. There are some people—including my wife—I'd like to talk it over with. But I'll be in touch with you tomorrow. Or, Sunday at the latest. Are you staying in New York over the weekend?"

"What . . . oh, yes. Yes, I think so. I'll look forward to hearing from you, Gilligan. And I hope that your answer will be yes."

But Howard Vandevanter looked drained. He made no real effort to detain his guests with courtesies—or anything else.

"Are you going to take it?" asked Charlie when they were crossing the lobby once again.

"It's an opportunity," Gilligan told him obliquely.

There was more than one way to interpret this, so Charlie responded in kind.

"Well, for God's sake, Leo, watch your step!"

16

To no one's surprise, Leo Gilligan took the job. By Monday morning, he was sitting in Amory Shaw's chair. Three days later the first returns were in.

"I knew Leo was smart, but I didn't realize he was that smart," they were saying in the coffee shop on John Street.

The president of the Cocoa Exchange was more parochial.

"I guess we can relax now." Wayne Glasscock heaved a gargantuan sigh of relief. "Thank God the bloodbath is over, although Gilligan certainly didn't take the line I expected."

Gene Orcutt could have told him why. He had drifted downstairs from his own quarters to give the Purchasing Division the benefit of his analysis.

"We pulled this one out of the bag by the skin of our teeth," he said grandly. "There were moments when even I was worried, and I know a lot of people are still confused about Leo's tactics."

It was the wrong note to strike. On the fifth floor, the cocoa buyers had been working double shifts since Dick Frohlich's death.

"But not you, I suppose," mocked Stratton. "Gilligan was consulting with you every inch of the way."

"Maybe not, but I'll tell you one thing he did," Orcutt replied sturdily. "He never forgot who he was working for. He didn't set out to steady the market for a bunch of speculators. He bought at the right rate to do Dreyer the most good."

The applause soon spread from John Street to the rest of the financial world. Bartlett Sims, Tom Robichaux, and Walter Bowman all removed their attention from Union Funding long enough to comment. By Thursday Charlie Trinkam was congratulating John Thatcher.

"The way I hear it, Gilligan is the best thing that's happened to Dreyer in a long time."

Thatcher's frown should have been warning enough. He was standing in a corner of his office, jamming folders into an overnight case.

"I am always happy to be of service to a client," he began with savage precision.

Charlie was big-hearted to a fault, but he favored a strict construction of the Sloan's obligations. "If it comes to that, Dreyer isn't a client," he said.

Thatcher refused to be sidetracked. ". . . or to the beneficiary of a trust for which I am responsible," he swept on. "I will gladly help with locating key personnel, suggesting new credit sources, or reviewing financial statements. *But . . .*"

"Yes?" asked Charlie, spellbound.

"*But* asking me to dance attendance on Etruscan vases is going too far."

Charlie opened his mouth, swallowed, and began again. "I can see how it would be," he said, keeping a firm grip on himself. "Is that the vase I read about in the *Times?*"

"The same," barked Thatcher. "And it is now dragging

me two hundred miles away from an overcrowded desk."

This was clearly no time for ribald sallies. Charlie proceeded with caution. "I thought the big shindig was here in New York this weekend. They said the Italian ambassador was coming and the governor of New York. And the Pope, too, for all I know."

The immediate crisis was past. Thatcher was not going to boil over. He even unbent sufficiently to explain. "The formal ceremonies are going ahead as planned. But, at the last minute, they discovered that the American insurance does not cover traveling. So the Italians have to pick up the vase at the museum. Apparently that is unthinkable without the presence of every living Dreyer trustee."

Charlie shook his head sadly. "I can see why."

The Etruscan vase had become headline news six months ago when some busybody discovered that one of Rome's countless missing art objects was on display at the Dreyer Museum. The curator responsible for the acquisition was deeply shocked and insisted on telling the world how the purchase had been made in the best of faith. Bills of sale were flourished, diplomatic notes exchanged, and negotiators appointed. While governments on both sides of the Atlantic tottered, while handwriting experts testified, the basic impasse remained unresolved. Italy never questioned the curator's status as a bona-fide purchaser, but it wanted its vase back. The museum never questioned Italy's moral right to the vase, but it wanted its money back. Finally two Milanese industrialists had appeared on the scene, haloed in light and dowered with gold. *Basta!* they cried. We will buy the vase for what it cost the museum.

"Well, you can't blame them," Charlie said fair-mindedly. "Somebody probably put the arm on them at a dinner party in Milan and, before they knew it, they were shelling out."

"Far from blaming them, I have the utmost sympathy for those two," Thatcher retorted. "At least for me the end is in sight. I understand the Italian authorities have a number of celebrations planned in Rome and Florence."

"Then let's hope that they're real culture hounds."

If so, they were hiding it admirably. It did not take Thatcher long to distinguish the two Italians once he arrived in Dreyer. Dr. Mercado was vigorous and bustling, with a fluent, not to say vernacular, command of the English language. Signor Alizio moved to a different drummer. He was slow and formal, speaking meticulously correct English. In spite of these dissimilarities, both gentlemen seemed at a loss as various Dreyer officials exerted themselves during the free period before the presentation. Curators, musical directors, and administrators jostled each other to lay at the feet of their visitors the enticements of art, music, and medicine. Curiously, it was Signor Alizio who broke through the barrage with a countersuggestion.

"You understand," he said apologetically, "we have La Scala in Milan, we have the Uffizi in Florence. We would like to take advantage of the unique opportunities here in Dreyer."

"Yes, yes," cried several of his listeners, all too willing to meet the challenge. There would be no opera and no Renaissance altar pieces, they promised. By a happy coincidence the chamber ensemble was practicing at this very instant a twelve-tone . . .

"That was not precisely what I had in mind," Alizio began, only to be drowned out by the claims of an exhibition of cubism and a breakthrough in cardiac research.

Dr. Mercado decided they were not communicating. Raising his voice over the clamor, he said: "Why not show us your cocoa plant?"

At this astonishing demand, his tormentors fell back, stupefied. One of them was ill-advised enough to protest: "But you can see that sort of thing anywhere!"

"For instance?" Mercado rapped back.

It was enough to bring Curtis Yeoman forward. "Of

course, we'd be delighted to show you through the plant. Howard, could we set that up for tomorrow morning?"

Experience had taught Vandevanter to be wary with guests of the Leonard Dreyer Trust. "Is there any special aspect of Dreyer that interests you?" he asked cautiously.

The flood gates opened. Dr. Mercado had the linguistic edge, but Signor Alizio compensated with his dogged persistence.

"Yes, yes, Umberto, rates of depreciation are most interesting. But the critical factor in all food processing must be quality control. Now the problem we have with tomato soup in my cannery—"

"Cannery?" Vandevanter's head lifted alertly.

Dr. Mercado was proud to describe his companion's achievements. "Giorgio owns the largest cannery in Italy. It may not be as big as Campbell's"—here Mercado's teeth flashed in a ferocious grin—"but it's not so small either."

"The Common Market and the growing demand for Mediterranean foods . . ." Alizio said earnestly.

"How you guys manage your inventory control . . ." Mercado bayed.

". . . a new bar that we've just finished standardizing," Vandevanter droned.

A magic circle was clearing around the participants. The devotees of higher culture, to a man, disassociated themselves from a conversation so blatantly commercial. Only one outsider intruded himself.

"The Dreyer bar is the result of a very simple process," Curtis Yeoman said kindly. "After all, milk chocolate is produced with a few natural ingredients."

Whatever his motive, he had miscalculated.

"I have heard people say the same thing about my tomato soup," Alizio murmured.

"If it's so simple, why have fortunes been spent trying to imitate it?" asked Mercado jovially.

Vandevanter beamed at his guests. They were turning out to be men after his own heart. "Why don't we go over to the plant right now?" he invited. "There's plenty of time."

To John Thatcher the next step was obvious. Here were three men yearning for mixing vats, conching rollers, and conveyor belts. Two of them had bought the right to ask for what they wanted; the third was in a position to deliver. He was already reaching for his coat when he was puzzled to hear Governor Yeoman raise one objection after another. It was rushing things with dinner in two hours, it was a shame to miss the medical center, and, finally, it was possible they might be part of a crowd if their visit was not scheduled.

"You see," he explained to the Italians, "we sometimes admit the public, and there may be tourists today."

"Sometimes! We have a guided tour every working day of the year!" The president of Dreyer was outraged. "Hundreds of thousands of people visit our plant every year. And they all love it!"

Within half an hour it was clear that, no matter what happened on other days, this particular tour was an unqualified success. The tourists loved it. Signor Alizio and Dr. Mercado loved it. And much to his surprise, John Thatcher found it engrossing.

The Howard Vandevanter who summarily dismissed the official guide was not the Howard Vandevanter one saw in New York. He might not know much about cocoa futures or commodity brokers, but he knew everything about the production and sale of Dreyer bars. What had been billed as the regular three o'clock tour rapidly escalated into a cram course on how to run a chocolate factory. With Signor Alizio leading the way, the tourists soon stopped ooh-ing and ah-ing over vats of cocoa butter and began to pelt their host with questions. How many pounds of sugar went into a thousand Dreyer bars? What did those machines cost? Which unions were represented on the line? Why were the conching rollers made of granite?

Vandevanter met them more than halfway. He was ready to tell them everything; he was ready to show them everything; if necessary, he was ready to roll up his sleeves and do everything. His enthusiasm was infectious. Before long two teenagers, who had started as conscripts in a family party, were showing signs of dedicating their lives to milk chocolate.

Throughout this virtuoso display, only one face registered consistent disapproval. Governor Yeoman was not the man to applaud success achieved by others. To make matters worse, he twice was saved from public humiliation when innocent bystanders, misled by his proprietarial air, addressed questions to him. Each time Howard Vandevanter good-naturedly intervened. But good-natured or not, he implied that mere trustees did not have these facts at their fingertips.

"What do you do to the beans in there?" a tourist asked, pausing by the revolving cylinders.

Yeoman tried to take refuge in generalities. "You see, before the cocoa beans can be used, they have to be cleaned."

"And roasted," Vandevanter took over. "The air in those cylinders is heated to more than four hundred degrees. What many people don't realize is that the cooling process is just as important as the heating. If you'll come over here . . ."

One of the teenage converts was responsible for Yeoman's second embarrassment. "I think I understand how we got this far," he said, brow wrinkled in furious concentration. "The beans are crushed between millstones to get chocolate liquor. Then you blend in milk and evaporate it to produce this dry stuff. But now you say you add more cocoa butter to make it into a paste. Well, where does the extra butter come from? We used up all there was in the beans."

He concluded by looking trustingly at the ex-governor of Pennsylvania. There was a long silence.

"Er . . . the beans, you understand, are broken up into nibs," Yeoman flailed about wildly, "and they have a very high cocoa butter content . . ."

"Fifty-five percent," the teenager offered helpfully.

Yeoman rolled his eyes.

"A lot of people are confused by that," said Vandevanter with kindly encouragement. "They forget we have more than one product. It's true we used up all the butter in the chocolate process. But we took out more than half of it when we were making cocoa powder. That's where the extra comes from."

After that, Governor Yeoman was abandoned as a source of information by the tour party, and his temper deteriorated rapidly.

"This is a ridiculous waste of time," he grumbled to Thatcher. "The president of Dreyer should have more important things to do than dragging a pack of tourists through the plant."

"He seems to do it very well," Thatcher said mildly. He even refrained from asking why dragging two unwilling Italians through an exhibition of cubism was a superior deployment of presidential energies.

Yeoman snorted. "Howard likes throwing his weight around, that's the simple truth of the matter. You've heard what he's doing about Gilligan's replacement."

Thatcher halted in midstride by the refining machines. "I didn't know there was one."

"There isn't yet. But when I asked him what he was doing about it, he said he was working on a list of possibles. He doesn't expect to reach a decision for several weeks, because it's so important to get the right man." Yeoman gave a short laugh. "You can see what he's up to. The right man for Howard will be the one who'll take his orders. We can kiss good-by to any independence for the New York operation now. Howard won't back down with a new man the way he did with Amory Shaw."

"He won't have to." Thatcher had started to march forward briskly. "Like it or not, the whole ball game has changed. The new man will be hired by Vandevanter and act accordingly—at least at the beginning. I don't suppose Amory Shaw was quite so regal during his first year or two with Dreyer."

Thatcher deliberately terminated the conversation, but

not without a passing thought. This was the first he had heard about Vandevanter backing down. Presumably the confrontation between him and Shaw had stopped short of open warfare. Yet, in all the swirl of rumor about the murder of Amory Shaw, Yeoman had chosen to keep this information to himself. It would be interesting to know why.

He caught up with his group at the packaging facilities in time to witness the first disappointment to mar the afternoon.

"But they're not gold!" burst out Dr. Mercado, shocked.

Indeed, they were not. The bars whizzing past had wrappers in brilliant red, white, and blue.

"These are our new Old Glory bars," explained Vandevanter. "We brought them out in time for the Bicentennial."

Such reasoning had little appeal for citizens of Milan. Signor Alizio, who was still trying to establish product identification for his can of tomato soup, was appalled. "But is this wise? The whole world thinks of the Dreyer bar as gold."

"Just wait six months," Vandevanter promised, "and they'll all know about Old Glory, too. It's going over with a bang in the domestic market. We're already revising our production goals. By the end of this quarter we expect to be one million over estimate. By the end of the next quarter . . ."

17

They were engaged in heavy counting at places other than Dreyer, New York.

"Well, we've racked up the commissions, I'll say that much," announced Jim Mears, "but I still wouldn't want to live through these past two weeks again."

He had thrown his notes on the table before sprawling in a chair, in loose-jointed fatigue.

Russ Martini cast a lackluster eye over his partner's figures. "It looks good to me," he finally said as if the effort of talking were too much for him. "But, boy, I'll be glad when the weekend comes."

The crisis in cocoa was over, but it had left behind men drawn with the strain and tension of continuous tightrope walking. They were not in the best condition to deal with howls from panic-stricken customers and mountains of paper work.

"You're coming back to the office tonight, aren't you?" Mears asked vaguely, as if this had not been settled hours ago.

"Mmm," agreed Martini. "I'll grab a bite somewhere and try to put in a couple of hours on those special accounts. I called Fran and told her I'd be staying in town tonight . . ."

Mears' nodding was as mechanical as Martini's speech. All paper work has to be cleared at commodity exchanges if trading the next day is to be permitted. Even in placid weeks it was not unusual for one of the partners to put in late hours. During critical periods, they alternated the swing shift like clockwork. It was not Russ Martini's plans for a working evening that kept the two men talking.

Partly it was an exhausted reluctance to move. But the real brake was the garrison mentality always produced by a sustained siege. The survivors have forged a desperate camaraderie out of shared suffering. Who else knows enough to afford support and sympathy? Who else wants to rake over every insignificant coal?

Russ Martini and Jim Mears had done as much coal raking as anybody in the building, but they were still at it.

"You notice who's missing from the list?" asked Mears, going on before Martini could finish his inspection. "Leo Gilligan, that's who!"

"But we had all his Dreyer business. And God knows there was enough of it, the way he strung things out. The guy must be a sadist."

Mears was shaking his head. "All the Dreyer business, and not one cent of his personal trading. Or are you going to tell me there wasn't any?"

"So he wanted to keep his accounts separate. What right do we have to complain? We got the lion's share." Still leaning over the list, Martini raised a hand to scrub his knuckles along the nape of his neck. "God, I can't remember being so tired."

"Well then, see you tomorrow," said Mears, finally bestirring himself. "Are you going out now?"

"What's that?" Martini had lowered a finger to pinpoint one item. "I just noticed this. No, you go along. There's one call I want to put through. It'll be a pleasure after the others I've had to make."

Eleanor Corwin put down the phone and turned to her husband. "We've just made twelve thousand three hundred dollars," she announced.

Rodger blinked. Five minutes ago he had returned from work, kissed his wife, and left her to answer the phone while he hung up his coat.

"If you can do that any old time," he asked cautiously, "why are we carrying this great big mortgage?"

She grinned mischievously. "Don't you want to know how I did it?"

"Maybe I'd be better off not knowing," Rodger suggested, with visions of himself in some future witness box.

"Oh, for heaven's sake! It was Dick. Don't you remember that broker's statement Mr. Shaw told us to give to the lawyer? Well, it was the broker who called just now."

Rodger relaxed. "Twelve thousand dollars?" he repeated, wanting to get the number right. "It didn't look as if it was worth that much."

"Mr. Martini, that's the broker, said it was a fluke. The cocoa market has been behaving oddly."

Rodger was not much interested in the explanation. "Say," he said, as one who has made a great discovery, "we could buy a boat!"

"Or," said Eleanor, following him like lightning, "we could go to Spain next summer."

"And you said you wanted to join that tennis club—"

". . . the kitchen positively has to be remodeled."

After an hour of pleasurable activity, Rodger Corwin looked up from his total in comical dismay. "That comes to slightly over forty-seven thousand dollars," he remarked.

He was not the only mathematician in the family.

"Then we're thirty-five thousand dollars short," Eleanor retorted crisply.

Rodger flinched. "What do you mean by that?" he demanded.

He did not receive an immediate answer. His wife's eyes were fixed on some distant horizon, but he could almost hear the wheels clicking.

"Of course, I took down Mr. Martini's address and phone number," she said, suddenly all business.

By now they were established on the sofa, with drinks on the coffee table. Rodger tried to remember how strong he had made them.

"Eleanor—" he began warningly, but to no avail.

"All that Dick did was buy some cocoa," she continued with alarming rationality. "And it isn't as if you have to pay out a lot of money. Mr. Martini told me that you just have to put up a tiny percentage. So, with twelve thousand dollars—"

Firmly Rodger Corwin removed his wife's glass. "Honey, I can see that glint in your eye. But just remember this, a lot of people lose money in cocoa, too."

The surprised delight in Eleanor Corwin's voice plus the prospect of a new customer provided Russ Martini with enough steam to rise from his chair and leave the office. At the Gaslight Lounge on Broad Street he found himself sharing a table, and reliving his latest coup.

"Of course, I'm going to have to explain to her about margin calls. But, if you ask me, that never really sinks in with some people."

Martini drained his beer thirstily and signaled for another, after the obligatory glance across the table. But Gene Orcutt was not making any progress through his Löwenbräu.

"And I don't just mean beginners," Martini warmed to his theme. "There are people who have been trading through me for years, people who'll talk you to death about the leverage they get in commodities, people who go crazy about how much percentage profit they can make on a small investment—well these same people sang a different tune when I called them last week and told them to ante up. They acted like they'd never heard of a margin call."

Orcutt forced a smile. "Yeah," he said dully, "I suppose you see a lot of that sort of thing."

Russ Martini was too tired to notice. "I get a bellyful," he answered succinctly. "And if you threaten to sell out these loudmouths, you should hear them. Suddenly you're taking bread from their children. It never occurs to them that it works the other way, too."

"But you do carry some of them, don't you?" asked

Orcutt, lifting his eyes for the first time. "I mean, even after you've said you're going to dump their holdings?"

"It depends on the customer, and it depends on the market. If I know a guy is good for it and the market isn't going crazy, sure I'll hang on a while. But the way things have been recently, there was no time for that kind of decision. Jim and I can't carry the whole world."

"Sure," Orcutt agreed too quickly. "You're not supposed to be running a charity."

The second beer, and the waitress approaching with a menu, were combining to mellow Martini. "We'd have to be the Ford Foundation to save every lamebrain in the cocoa market," he said roundly. "You eating here?"

"What?" For a moment, Orcutt was lost. Then he shook his head. "No, I'll be pushing off home in a couple of minutes. But now that cocoa has touched bottom and is on the way up, things aren't so bad for your customers any more. Even if you sell some of their holdings, they'll make money on what's left."

Deep in a choice between lamb chops and pork chops, Martini mistook a plea for reassurance for a search for instruction.

"Depends what the poor saps bought at," he replied absently. "They may not have anything left. Anyway, who knows what cocoa is going to do? We may be in for another slide."

"Another slide?" said a reproachful voice. "You should have more faith in me, Russ."

It was Leo Gilligan, halting by their table on his way out. He gave every evidence of having finished a profitable day with an appropriate celebration. Here, at least, was one trader who had escaped the prevailing aura of anxiety. He declined an invitation to sit. No, he said, he was just passing the time of day.

"But not handing out any information, is that it, Leo?" Martini asked resignedly.

"Now, Russ, I put Dreyer back into the market, didn't I? What more do you want from me in one week?" Gilligan's shrewd eyes examined the broker.

"I want all I can get," Martini said frankly. But he had been reminded of a fact. "Say, Leo, while you were putting Dreyer back in the market, you didn't forget to put yourself back in, did you?"

Smiling, Gilligan said: "That's classified information. Let's say I like to keep a watertight wall between Leo Gilligan and Dreyer's man on the floor."

Martini had to settle for this. "I'll say this for you, Leo," he conceded, "you came through on your margin calls last week like a real gent."

"It's all part of the game." Gilligan gestured expansively with his cigar. "But take it all in all, the ups and the downs, the Cocoa Exchange is a great place."

"We've decided that the Cocoa Exchange simply doesn't meet our requirements," Craig Phibbs told the phone sternly. "We need action, we need excitement, we need a spectacle that can grip millions of people."

"I thought this was for educational television," said Wayne Glasscock, confused.

"Public television is reaching a larger audience every day. The networks are already very worried. And in view of our responsibilities, we can't afford anything second-rate. So we're dropping your Exchange in favor of a broader panorama."

"That's too bad," said Glasscock cheerfully. "Of course, I wish you the best."

"You may not like our film when it comes out," Phibbs warned. "It's going to cut pretty close to the bone."

"Oh, I think I'll survive," said Glasscock before signing off.

Phibbs leaned back in his swivel chair and waited for his entourage's reaction.

"You sure told him," said a young man admiringly.

"He deserved it." Sonia Libby was quite heated. "That was some kind of cooperation they gave us. I hope you're going to let Eve Glasscock know how you feel."

"There's nothing to get excited about," soothed Phibbs, every inch the white hunter. "Things are going to turn out much better this way. With my new plans we're going to expose the whole money establishment. Oh, sure, everybody who counts already knows intellectually the greed and avarice that motivate the men who control this country. But they don't feel it in their gut. My film is going to get to them like a kick in the stomach. Intellect won't have anything to do with it."

"I think you're making the right decision, Craig," said his second-in-command judiciously.

Phibbs ignored him. "By the time I'm done, my audience will see that unscrupulous hunger to make a buck, they'll hear it, they'll damn well taste it and smell it!"

His followers were rapt.

"This is going to be bigger than public television," Craig decided, closing his eyes to view the future. "Natually we'll wrap up PBS. Every station will buy the rights. Then the commercial boys won't be able to stand it. Not when they see the ratings. The seepage will start in the big Eastern cities. They're always the bellwethers. New York and Boston and Washington. We'll move into the big time and start getting Johnny Carson prices. Before you know it, we'll be sweeping commercial TV like a tidal wave."

"Just like Julia Child!" cried the young man excitedly.

"No," Phibbs frowned. "Not like Julia Child. . . . What's this?"

The girl who entered might have been carrying the good news from Ghent to Aix. She did not quite fall down at the emperor's feet as she deposited a large manila envelope.

"They've developed your shots from over at the Cocoa Exchange," she said breathlessly.

Phibbs waved them away. "Put them in a basket. I've got no time for them now. Who cares about the Cocoa Exchange?" He laughed sardonically. "When you get right down to it, they're just the first step in a bunch of candy bars."

*　　*　　*

Fred Nagle took a different view of the place of the candy bar in modern America. He had just received the latest batch of orders from his despised son-in-law.

"If they'll buy Old Glory from him, they'll buy it from anybody," he told his wife, gloating over the figures.

Helen knew her duty. "Oh, he's not so bad," she said without enthusiasm.

But Fred's remark had been pro forma. Hereafter he would make it sound as if Old Glory was running around to the outlets by itself.

"They can't keep it in stock," he said jubilantly, "and you know what? Ted Kanelos tells me it's the whole country, not just the Northeast."

The Nagles had revised their first opinion of Madison Avenue. Now they were calling it up every day to get the latest news.

"What did he say?" asked Helen.

"The most successful advertising campaign in the history of Bridges, Gray & Kanelos. Already they're taking action up in Dreyer. By the end of this quarter they expect to be over estimate. And by the end of next quarter . . ."

18

In Dreyer, meanwhile, the Etruscan vase was changing hands. This transaction did not come a minute too soon for John Thatcher, who by now was surfeited with elaborate, graceful allusions to how great art transcends national boundaries.

Dr. Mercado and Signor Alizio, more inured to eloquence for its own sake, stood up to their ordeal well. Dr.

Mercado, in fact, gave back better than he got, flooring the assembled dignitaries with the recital of a long, no doubt appropriate, portion of *The Divine Comedy.*

"Presso a color, che non veggon pur l'opra . . . Ma per entro i pensier miran col senno . . ."

Naturally the subsequent rush to the bar assumed stampede proportions. It was not until they had drinks in hand that Thatcher realized conching rollers were not Dreyer's only current attraction for the Italians.

"The hospitality of the Dreyer Company is most munificent," Signor Alizio began. "They have provided us with quarters in the Staatskill Hotel."

"They've given us the biggest damned suite I've ever seen," Dr. Mercado supplemented, with a descriptive sweep of his arms that imperiled a passing tray. "Anybody would think we represented Nestlé's."

They were even more important than that, Thatcher reminded them. Their generosity was sparing the Dreyer Museum a lawsuit, and the company was duly grateful.

"Not at all, not at all," both Italians disclaimed politely before relapsing into gloom.

"Everything is just as it should be," said Alizio, allowing a wistful note to creep into his voice. "It is merely that . . ."

"Yes?" encouraged Thatcher.

Mercado took a deep breath. "We wanted to be in the other hotel." Seeing the bewilderment on Thatcher's face, he amplified. "The one where the murder happened."

Thatcher should have known. While their hosts had been reading the *Proceedings of the Royal Society* and *Art Annual,* the Milanese had been devouring the popular press. For the first time it looked as if the Sloan could make a meaningful contribution to the current festivities.

"I myself am staying at the Royal Dutch Motel," he explained. "Perhaps we could slip quietly away from here and have a drink in my room?"

*   *   *

As they passed under the lighted archway, Thatcher realized at once that his luck was in. The inner courtyard was deserted except for one lone figure. It was not the criminal revisiting the scene of his crime. It was Captain Huggins of the Dreyer police.

Thatcher revealed his mission at once. "Good evening, Captain. I was about to show Dr. Mercado and Signor Alizio here where Dick Frohlich was murdered."

The captain took his responsibility toward guests of the company as seriously as everyone else in town did.

"I was just brushing up on the geography myself," he admitted. "The pool is where Frohlich was finished off, but it's the rest of the setup that's interesting."

Two pairs of intelligent dark eyes absorbed the basic facts quickly.

"There is only one entrance to this courtyard," Alizio announced after a moment's survey. "The way we have just come."

"More or less," Huggins agreed. "If you don't count the rooms themselves."

As the tenant of one of those rooms on the night of the murder, Thatcher appreciated the implications of the captain's accuracy.

"You did say that there were signs the murderer waited in ambush here somewhere, didn't you, Captain?" he asked.

"Someone sure as hell did. Over in those bushes." Captain Huggins led the way to a tall clump of ornamental shrubbery lying in deep shadow. "You'd be practically invisible here, so long as you kept quiet. No need to worry about being spotted by people returning to their rooms or looking out the window. But at the same time—"

He was not allowed to continue. Dr. Mercado had entered the spirit of things by diving into the rhododendrons and taking his own line of sight. "Yes, that lantern over the archway acts like a spotlight. You could recognize your victim the minute he stepped under it—and have plenty of time to sneak up behind him."

Signor Alizio had remained decorously on the paved

walk, but he was still an enthusiastic collaborator in the reconstruction.

"It might not be necessary to move at all, Umberto," he said, staring somberly at the courtyard. "It would be dependent on the victim's movements."

Huggins nodded as if he were dealing with promising rookies. "That's right. Frohlich's room was on the same side as those bushes, so his path took him right in front of that rhododendron. In fact he fell into it when he was slugged. If you look closely, you can still see some of the broken branches."

But Latin zeal was tempered by fastidiousness. Instead of accepting the captain's invitation, Mercado removed himself from the site of the attack, dusted his hands, and faced the pool. "Poor guy! I suppose he was dumped in there, and then the murderer beat it."

Thatcher had no hesitation in agreeing with the final conclusion. "After all, no matter how careful the murderer was, there must have been a certain amount of noise. He couldn't be sure that someone wouldn't look out."

"The odds were in his favor," Huggins argued. "We've talked to every occupant of this courtyard. They were all home before Frohlich and they had all gone to bed. At that hour and with every light turned off, the murderer didn't have to worry too much. He could figure on at least a minute's head start, and that would be enough to get out of the courtyard, back to where his car was."

"He couldn't know that everyone was home," Thatcher objected. "Not unless he'd studied the motel's registration book. And that isn't likely, if he was the same one telephoning hotels to find out where Frohlich was spending the night."

Huggins fell back on his long experience. "So he took a chance. Most murderers do. But he was pretty safe. It was after one by the time that poker game broke up. And Dreyer isn't New York City. The hamburger joints stay open an hour after the last movie, and then everybody goes to bed."

"We had noticed how your community has . . . er . . .

escaped metropolitan pressures," said Signor Alizio dolefully. It had taken only twenty-four hours in the hinterland for his opinion of Milan to skyrocket.

Dr. Mercado hastened to assure Captain Huggins that no disparagement of his community was intended. "It's a great little town," he said insincerely, before diverting the conversation, "but you said something about the killer going back to his car. How do you figure that?"

"It took a lot of questioning, but we've finally established that there was a car parked by the restaurant, when the help went home at midnight. It wasn't there at six o'clock the next morning."

"Do you have a description of the car?" Thatcher tried to keep everything but mild curiosity from his voice.

"About what you'd expect." Huggins shrugged. "It was a late model Chevy sedan, dark color. We got that much from one of the busboys, and we're lucky he was that specific."

Huggins was looking pleased enough to suggest that no member of the Dreyer front office was associated with such a vehicle. Thatcher himself, remembering the vast white Oldsmobile in which Howard Vandevanter arrived for work, was conscious of relief.

The Italians were happily unaware of these crosscurrents. "Your discovery is interesting, of course," said Alizio courteously. "But it does not appear to be very helpful—an unknown car and an unknown driver."

"You'd be surprised," Huggins rejoined. "A car's not a little thing. If the killer was saddled with it at one o'clock in the morning, he had to do something with it. It hasn't turned up in Dreyer. And there are just so many ways out of Dreyer."

Alizio was puzzled by Huggins' newfound dogmatism, but not so John Thatcher. Murder was probably a novelty to the captain but, like every policeman in the country, he was an expert on traffic patterns, hit-and-run drivers, stolen-car rings, and youthful joy riders. For him the darker motivations of latter-day Cains might be unknown territory, but he knew what anyone would do behind a steering wheel under any conceivable set of circumstances.

"Always supposing that was the murderer's car," Thatcher finished his thoughts aloud.

"Oh, I could be wrong," Huggins agreed readily. "But until someone shows me a better bet, I'm assuming the murderer did a bunch of things." Three muscular fingers were extended, ready to be ticked off. "I say he was the one who called the hotels to locate Frohlich, he was the one who waited in the bushes, and he was the one who drove away that car. Any other way you look at it means a whole bunch of people circling around Frohlich's murder, doing crazy things and not coming forward because they have something to hide. I don't buy that unless I have to."

Signor Alizio seemed to accept the principle of narrowing things down. In fact, he had a suggestion along these lines. "But you have ascertained the time at which these events occurred. Surely that must eliminate some suspects."

"Oh, I wouldn't call them suspects." The Dreyer police chief looked shocked. "We've asked a few discreet questions. But, like I said, it was one o'clock after a big business banquet. Everybody claims they were asleep. As for wives, most of them went to bed early and left their husbands to find the Alka-Seltzer by themselves."

Dr. Mercado refused to be drawn by this insight into American domestic manners. "I don't see how you can cross off anything at this stage. Until you know the motive for the murder, you can't tell how many different people might be involved."

"We haven't forgotten that. And the New York City boys have been a big help. But so far it's all negative. They had their auditors run a ruler over Frohlich's department down there."

"Ah, these American audits," breathed Alizio respectfully. "We have heard of them. They are performed on your criminals, and on your politicians—and apparently even on your victims."

"Well, this one didn't do much good. The buyer's department came out clean as a whistle. And even Frohlich's private trading account was just what I'd expected. No big surprises for anyone, or even little ones, either."

Thatcher's attention had been captured by one phrase. "Did you see the account summary yourself, Captain?" he asked.

"Sure thing. Asked them to send it down to me." Huggins grinned at Thatcher's response. "I probably understood it better than most of the boys down there. I take a little flyer myself, every now and then. Here in Dreyer, we're all pretty interested in cocoa."

"I should have realized that," said Thatcher. He should not have been misled by Captain Huggins' man-in-the-street act. In a pinch the local police force was probably capable of running the whole conching process, too. Huggins' area of expertise might be a little odd but he was a specialist quite as much as anyone in the New York Homicide Division. And he was also far too busy to waste time on visitors, no matter how eminent. The only question was when he would demand his *quid pro quo.*

He did so immediately.

"I hear you were at the Cocoa Exchange yourself, Mr. Thatcher, when Amory Shaw was knifed. Now, I've seen the reports but that isn't the same as an eyewitness. I was wondering . . ."

Fifteen minutes later Thatcher felt as if he had been mauled by an exceptionally powerful vacuum cleaner. He re-created for Huggins everything seen, heard, or sensed from that perch in the visitors' gallery.

"Unbelievable," said Huggins at the tale's conclusion. "Well, we wanted to know why someone killed Dick Frohlich. Now we know the answer's right on John Street." He paused to let his eyes stray across the highway to the compound of the Dreyer Chocolate Company. "In one sense, anyway."

19

Combine an Etruscan vase with Columbus Day, and the prospects are not good. John Thatcher had been unhopeful but, by Sunday afternoon, he had to admit it could have been worse. The cocktail party was being held in the garden of the Museum of Modern Art. Benign weather over the three-day weekend operated on midtown Manhattan like a giant pump, sucking away population, traffic, and pollution. A blue sky arched overhead, a gentle breeze rustled the gallant city trees, and the air smelled fresh and clean. With some satisfaction Thatcher reflected that every resort within a hundred and fifty miles was currently the scene of traffic congestion, choking exhaust fumes, and irritable crowds. Nor was he alone in his sense of well-being. There was no doubt that the museum's party was going with a bang. The guests had come for duty and remained for pleasure. The courtyard was filled with animated chattering groups. Lavish supplies of food and drink were holding up well. And, considering the nature of the occasion, there was some unexpectedly interesting conversation to be had.

Of course, not everyone was hitting it lucky. On the other side of the buffet, Curtis Yeoman seemed to be stuck with the governor of New York. And Howard Vandevanter's yellow head, silhouetted against some angular sculpture, was more golden than ever under kleig lights. Bridges, Gray & Kanelos was immortalizing the moment for a future commercial. But Thatcher himself had just emerged from an account of dark doings at the Brooklyn

Museum. An employee of that venerable institution had described a recent dismissal.

"They threatened to eject him physically," the young man had reported.

"No!"

"Without any warning, you understand, they sent the head of security with a note telling him to leave forthwith!"

"What did he do?"

"What could he do? This guard is a great hulking brute. And that's not all."

"Ye-e-s?"

"He was wearing a uniform we didn't even know he had. Epaulettes and a gun belt. He looked like the embodiment of militarism. But I can tell you, we're not taking this lying down."

"I should hope not," Thatcher said warmly.

"We're going over the director's head. The petition is already eighty percent subscribed. And if the board doesn't see reason, why we'll just walk out." The young man squared his shoulders defiantly. "I'd like to see them try running that museum without us."

A carping mind might have found Thatcher's agreement ambiguous.

"So would I," he had said before walking away.

But the exchange had given him food for thought. Was the Sloan Guaranty Trust turning into a stagnant backwater? To the best of his knowledge—and he was in a position to know—when the Sloan told a man to go, he went quietly. Certainly no trust officer had ever been carried from the building, kicking and screaming. Was this good or bad?

A parting in the crowd brought him face to face with someone who might share his interest in this problem. Charlie Trinkam was carefully convoying two full glasses through the mob.

"What are you doing here?" asked Thatcher before the implications of the second glass registered. "Oh, I suppose you're squiring somebody."

Charlie grinned. "That isn't the way I'd put it myself. I think I'm being squired. But anyway, I'm with the television crew."

"Good God, don't you see enough advertising people in PR?"

"This isn't the advertising bunch. This is educational television. They're shooting some footage for one of their documentaries."

The ramifications of Charlie's extracurricular life never ceased to bemuse his colleagues. But at the moment Thatcher had other preoccupations. He retailed the Brooklyn Museum melodrama and put his own question.

"Everyone else seems to be having personnel troubles these days." Scrupulously he supported his statement with the list—colleges, hospitals, museums. Even the White House was not without its staff problems. "Is there something wrong with us?"

Charlie had his own explanation. "No, it's just that the new breed never considers working for a bank. If you want to keep in touch, John, come and meet Sonia."

Sonia was dressed in a flowing caftan, her dark hair was knotted into one long braid, and she was fighting the good fight before the introductions were completed.

". . . and, John, this is Mrs. Libby," Charlie was saying.

"M-z-z-z!" she interrupted fiercely.

"All right. M-z-z Libby," Charlie obligingly buzzed back.

Well, that settled it, thought Thatcher. The woman was going to be *you* as far as he was concerned. Nobody was committing him to a word that didn't have a vowel.

Charlie continued his pacification program. "John is one of the Dreyer trustees, handing over the vase."

He had struck a spark. Sonia Libby's gaze, conning the horizon for worthier entertainment, suddenly swiveled back to her companions.

"We could use you," she announced in a voice blending surprise and self-congratulation. So might a sultan have spoken who had come to examine the latest consignment

153

of houris without high hopes. She nodded to herself, then without warning aimed a single shriek into the crowd. "Craig!"

The call produced not one, but two, additions to their party. Craig Phibbs, complete with light meter, was accompanied by Dr. Umberto Mercado.

"Yes?" he asked impatiently.

It was Sonia's hour.

"I've got the face you were looking for. Look at those lines," she urged. "Think of the shadows we can get with the right lighting."

A slow, remorseless scrutiny began. For no reason at all, Thatcher found himself fighting the temptation to blink. Dr. Mercado watched indulgently. Charlie Trinkam had clearly decided to let the storm rage where it would.

After moments of suspense, Phibbs made his decision. "I like it." He addressed Thatcher. "This documentary is going to shake up the whole country. It's called *Greed,* and we'll be using you in one of the symbolic sequences."

Thatcher was under no illusion as to exactly what he was going to symbolize.

"I see it all." Phibbs was gripped by creative ecstasy. "We open with a facial study of you. You're introduced as a banker. Then we zoom in on the vase. You're toying with it callously. Your indifferent hands don't recognize its inherent worth."

Thatcher stiffened at this preposterous statement. Say what you will about bankers, they do not toy carelessly with breakables having an insurance cover of over a million dollars.

"Go on," he said evenly.

"Then you hand the vase to Dr. Mercado, here. He accepts it reverently, almost humbly. Meanwhile the sound-track is carrying your voice. You're talking about money. With this unique work of art in front of you, you can't see it, you're blind to it. It has no meaning for you. Instead you're reading the check Dr. Mercado has given you, thanking him for the two hundred thousand dollars but—"

"Two hundred and twenty-five thousand," Dr. Mercado corrected amiably.

It took more than facts to throw Craig Phibbs off stride. "These details don't matter. The important thing is that then we see Dr. Mercado's hands—fine, sensitive, tapering fingers caressing the curves of the vase, lingering over the swell of its body, feeling the rich glaze . . ."

His voice died away, seduced by his imagery. He was not the only one affected. Dr. Mercado had raised his squat, hairy hands and was examining them with deep interest. Then he shuddered.

"You don't catch me touching that thing," he said firmly. "What if I break it?"

Over the years Craig Phibbs had often encountered recalcitrance. He always did better ignoring it than reasoning with it.

"It's a lucky thing that you speak English so well. It would be a crying shame to have to dub on a masterpiece like this."

Even Italian amiability has its limits. "Why shouldn't I speak English well? I went to Rensselaer Polytech."

For an instant, Phibbs was shaken. He preferred his sensitive Continentals to have learned their English at Oxford. But he made an immediate recovery. "We don't have to mention it," he said.

Battle was joined on an unlikely issue. "Why shouldn't we mention it? Rensselaer is a first-class engineering school."

Thatcher was pleased to see that the Phibbs insulation was not entirely impenetrable.

"Look, we're pushing the fact that you're an artist, that you appreciate the intrinsic greatness of the vase, you respond instinctively. Why bring engineering into it?" Phibbs was almost shouting.

"I'm not an artist. I'm a capitalist."

There was a shocked silence. Four-letter abuse was common in Phibbs' circles—and in his films—but there were still words that he reacted to like a maiden aunt. Of course, he didn't hear them often.

"I thought you said you were Dr. Mercado," he said suspiciously.

"I am."

"What are you a doctor of?"

"I'm a doctor of electrical engineering. I make cathode ray tubes for television sets."

Phibbs' world was crashing around his ears, but he was still fighting. "You should have said so at the beginning. Here, I've been thinking you were a professor or a curator. It's a good thing we found out in time."

"I just told you," Mercado remarked.

But Phibbs preferred to think he had unmasked an impostor. "I'm afraid you won't do for *Greed*," he said curtly.

Thatcher felt the time was ripe to announce his own retirement from the cast. "I'm not the man you want at all. I have nothing to do with the presentation itself. You want to talk to Howard Vandevanter, over there. He's in charge at the Dreyer end."

Phibbs glanced over to the corner where Vandevanter had completed his duties by one set of television cameras.

"The fair-haired one?" Phibbs dismissed him out of hand. "No, I don't like the way he photographs. Yours is the face I want."

Thatcher was perversely annoyed. Why was he supposed to represent greed so much more compellingly than Vandevanter?

"Well, you can't have it. Maybe Vandevanter is more photogenic than you think."

Phibbs shook his head stubbornly. "No, he's the one I was telling the police about yesterday. They wanted to know about his fight with that guy who got murdered. I know what he looks like on camera."

A less self-centered man might have noticed the sudden stillness that enveloped their little group in the midst of the bustle about them. Glasses were tinkling, women were laughing, but Charlie Trinkam and John Thatcher had both frozen.

"What fight?" Thatcher asked at last.

A great artist learns that other people do not see the same essentials that he does. Phibbs knew that the world was filled with lesser men, distracted by the minutiae of life, failing to see the constant truths. When he wanted something, he could descend to their level.

"Just before the murder," he humored his listeners. "Sonia and I saw them on the seventh floor. We didn't pay any attention to what they were saying. But I was interested in their expressions."

"We just caught sight of them as we passed the end of their corridor," Sonia volunteered. "Craig said it was just the kind of vignette we wanted."

"Then you don't know exactly when you saw them?" Thatcher prodded.

Phibbs was bored, but still tolerant. "You understand I wasn't interested in them as people, only as plastic expressions of an emotion. But I snapped a view of them. It's the way I work."

His acolyte recognized her cue. "Craig takes stills as working notes. Just the way a painter does sketches, or a sculptor does models. He has whole files that he can consult when he's planning a creation." She sounded awestruck. "It was just an accident that this one included the clock."

John Thatcher and Charlie Trinkam were awestruck, too. This gave Phibbs his opportunity to end the digression. "So I know that Vandevanter won't do at all. He doesn't have the right planes."

Automatically, Thatcher fended off the renewed attack. It took some time to convince Craig Phibbs that *Greed* would have to be filmed without active assistance from the Sloan Guaranty Trust.

"You should have foisted him onto Yeoman," Charlie complained when they were alone. He had been champing at the bit for the last five minutes.

"I don't want him tying up Yeoman now," Thatcher retorted. "I want the field free and clear."

"Are you going to tell Yeoman about this?"

"No, I merely want to find out when Vandevanter arrived in New York. If he's been here all weekend . . ."

Charlie nodded comprehendingly. "Phibbs told his story to the cops yesterday. They would have tried to check with Vandevanter right away. If he was available and he got through a third degree okay, then Phibbs is blowing this up out of proportion. But if the police haven't seen Vandevanter yet, then anything may happen."

Thatcher agreed but felt constrained to add: "While I dislike saying a good word for Phibbs, you have to admit that he is certainly not trying to inflate the importance of his information."

"Hell, he doesn't even realize the importance of it," Charlie rejoined.

"I wonder why the police haven't had Phibbs' information before," Thatcher mused.

"I can think of a lot of good reasons. But one'll get you three that Phibbs forgot those stills until they were developed and turned up on his desk."

Agreeing, Thatcher maintained a steady course toward the buffet, where he was surprised to find Yeoman and the governor still at it.

"What do you think is keeping them together?" asked Charlie, ever curious. "The governor's art collection?"

"More likely Yeoman is demanding action on Shaw's murder."

They were both wrong. It was the Republican Party that was exercising these two politicians.

Thatcher held his interruption to a bare minimum, with one question.

"Howard?" Yeoman was undisturbed. "Have you been looking for him? He came here direct from the airport. And I'm afraid you've missed him. He left a couple of minutes ago."

"Well, that's that," Charlie summed up. "Let's have

one more drink and then find dinner somewhere while we're waiting for the axe to fall."

But they barely reached the bar. This time it was Yeoman who came in search of them.

"Thatcher, I just had a call from Howard. The police were waiting for him at his hotel." His eyes were blank with shock. "My God, they've arrested the president of Dreyer!"

20

"When I think of those articles I've read about how the law discriminates against the poor," Charlie was saying twenty-four hours later, "I'm tempted to dash something off myself."

Walter Bowman was always willing to keep the ball in play. "You mean something like—*Getting Arrested Ain't Fun Even If You're Rich?*"

"That's right."

"The only trouble," said Walter, the specialist, "is that Howard Vandevanter isn't really rich—"

"Rich enough," Charlie interrupted firmly. "And he's the president of the Dreyer Chocolate Company. That makes a nice contrast with the poor slob who can't afford to hire a lawyer."

Since this was indisputable, there ensued a few moments during which Thatcher idly reflected on his subordinates and their fortes. Bowman always stood ready to brandish statistics about income distribution and asset ownership in the United States; Charlie invariably took experience, assimilated it, and used it to enrich his already eclectic philosophy of life.

Still, there were times when somebody had to keep them on track.

"Don't forget," Thatcher said, "today's Columbus Day. That's been a contributing factor to Vandevanter's troubles."

"How could I?" Charlie replied with cause.

Other Americans might associate Columbus Day with parades, or closing cottages in the Berkshires, or breakdowns on the thruway of their choice. It was going to be a good many years before Thatcher and Charlie could equate it with anything but the heroics required to spring Howard Vandevanter, president of the Dreyer Chocolate Company, from the jug.

Yesterday's dash between the Museum of Modern Art and the lockup had been a miracle of speedy transport, but still a nightmare. At the time, as well as in retrospect, the nightmare had been largely of Curtis Yeoman's making.

"Howard getting himself arrested for murder!" he had repeated, first in confusion, then in fury. "My God, John, do you know what this is going to do to Dreyer? If you'd told me six months ago that any of this could have happened to us, I'd have called you a liar to your face. It's insanity, that's what it is."

Thatcher did not have time to ask if the governor was thinking ahead to possible legal defenses. At the precinct house, other questions took higher priority.

Howard Vandevanter had not been charged with murder. He had been booked, and was being held, for questioning.

The desk sergeant was courteous but unyielding.

"The only one who gets to see Vandevanter, Mr. . . . er . . . Youmans—"

"Yeoman!" Yeoman snapped. "I've already explained—"

"Yeoman." The sergeant would have agreed to anything. He was not even pretending to care. "You're not Vandevanter's lawyer, are you? Because he's the only one Captain Bruce told me to let in . . ."

Before Yeoman could try bearing down again, Thatcher interjected himself.

"Would it be possible for us to talk to the officer in charge?" he asked.

The calm, incurious inspector turned to him. Then: "Today's Sunday. And tomorrow's Columbus Day."

At the time, Thatcher had been too intent on deflecting Yeoman to take in the full significance of this. A clatter had made him turn to see what he knew in his bones must be the first of the press.

"Of course the police aren't taking the holiday off," he said sharply to Yeoman, who was still fulminating after being hustled outside. "Presumably, they are busy—trying to question Vandevanter, among other things."

"Escobedo and Miranda," crooned Charlie with a nice, tango beat.

"What we should do," said Thatcher, wondering why he had to say this to Yeoman, "is get hold of Vandevanter's lawyer."

This terminated Yeoman's first reaction to the arrest, which had struck Thatcher as more like a self-defeating tantrum than the response of a seasoned politician.

"Yes, of course," said Yeoman, glancing at his watch. "Let's go back to my hotel and get on the phone."

During the ride to the Waldorf, Charlie spotted a small ray of sunshine. "At least they haven't charged him with murder."

"The damned fool!" Yeoman ejaculated.

Charlie glanced at Thatcher and opted for silence. Frustration, anxiety, and fear can make one man say this of another, even where there is also affection and respect. Thatcher had heard fathers call their sons damned fools, and mean it for the moment—just because of the terrible depth of their concern and involvement. But Yeoman's bitterness was bleak. Thatcher had known he did not like Howard Vandevanter. He had not realized he hated him.

"If he was stupid enough to lie about that picture,"

Yeoman said harshly, "he's stupid enough to do anything."

"The sooner we get Vandevanter's lawyer, the better," Thatcher repeated.

It was easier said than done.

There was nobody at the Vandevanter home in Dreyer.

"That's fine," said Yeoman, jamming the receiver down. "Vandevanter's in jail and his family's out—"

"It's a holiday," Charlie reminded him shortly. "And Vandevanter's family didn't expect him to get arrested on this trip to New York. It's going to be a big shock when they read about it."

It took much to strain Charlie's large tolerance for his fellow man—but Yeoman was managing to do it.

"Try Dreyer's lawyer," Thatcher ordered.

Yeoman's face tightened. His professed ignorance of Vandevanter's personal attorney had already cost time in this abortive call to Mrs. Vandevanter. Now they were getting to the heart of the matter.

"Under the circumstances," he said stubbornly, "I don't think it would be proper for Dreyer's counsel to represent Vandevanter."

Thatcher had begun to suspect that something like this was coming. Charlie put it all in one pithy word.

"Bullshit," he said, without smiling.

Hastily, while the color mounted in Yeoman's cheeks, Thatcher amplified this, without blunting its thrust. "There may be a legitimate question about who should represent Vandevanter in any future legal actions," he said. "But at the moment, he is the president of the Dreyer Chocolate Company. Those are the circumstances under which we are operating, Yeoman."

He was not smiling either.

"I can't agree—"

Thatcher had never pretended to possess the lawyer's art of arguing ad infinitum. "If you are unwilling to cooperate," he said crisply, "I shall myself contact every member of the board of directors."

Under threat of *force majeure,* Yeoman yielded. He did so with bad grace. "Very well," he said, angrily reaching for the phone.

Once again, Columbus Day defeated them. Luther H. Barnett, Esq., counsel to the Dreyer Chocolate Company, was not at his home. There was, however, a voice.

Thatcher and Charlie afterward compared notes about the side of the conversation available to them. Thatcher's version—that Yeoman was talking for effect—was milder and probably less accurate than Charlie's: "He was faking it."

What Yeoman said was: ". . . out? Yes . . . yes. Well, will you tell him that Governor Yeoman will be calling him then? Fine." Downing the receiver, he explained: "The girl says that Barnett is away for the day. He's expected back tonight."

The fractional pause might have been taken as defiance. When Thatcher held his tongue, Yeoman continued: "I think the wisest course of action is for me to get up to Dreyer so I can talk directly to him."

"Fine," said Thatcher neutrally.

For all his experience, Yeoman could not keep a spark of triumph from his eyes. "Yes, that's the best idea. I think I'll go and get Barnett lined up. That should be the best way to satisfy our immediate needs."

Charlie nearly spoiled the whole thing by trying to nail him down. "'Do you intend to call John—or me—once you get hold of Barnett?" he asked.

"Certainly," said Yeoman, with dignity. "And now . . ."

They had barely reached the lobby before Charlie overflowed.

"I wouldn't hold my breath waiting for that call, would you, John?"

"No," said Thatcher. "But I think we might make more progress getting hold of somebody to help Vandevanter, with Yeoman off our hands."

They might have proceeded to a full discussion of Yeoman's behavior and the reasons for it but, at that moment, a burly man deposited the familiar bundle on the glass-topped newsstand. Thatcher and Charlie coincided with the wire cutter.

The *Post,* starved almost to emaciation by the holiday news shortage, had done what it could with what it had. There was only one hard fact—but it was set in a fat, black headline: DREYER PREXY ARRESTED.

"Come on," said Thatcher, heading for a telephone of his own.

The following hours were an eye-opener.

"My God!" said Charlie at one point. "Is the whole New York Bar on Fire Island?"

If they were not, they were on Martha's Vineyard. By the time Thatcher had gotten as far down his list as Stanton Carruthers—whose specialty was trusts and estates—he was heartily sick of offshore property from Georgia to Casco Bay.

"I should have foreseen it," he said irascibly. "With every Sloan lawyer apparently on Nantucket, it was only to be expected that Carruthers would be holed up on some piece of rock in the North Atlantic."

Charlie got up, stretched, and completed his arrangements to rendezvous with Thatcher next morning, before leaving on a sweet-and-sour note. "Just thank God that Irene Jackson likes the mountains," he advised.

Paul Jackson, a trial lawyer, was available in the sense that he was on the mainland. Getting his number in Sugar Hill, New Hampshire, then getting him, had proved arduous but worthwhile. He was going to be on tap first thing in the morning.

"Which reminds me," said Charlie, "our pal Yeoman didn't call, did he? What do you want to bet that he couldn't get in touch with Barnett, after all?"

"Right now," said Thatcher, "I'm not willing to bet on anything."

But bright and early Columbus Day, Paul Jackson arrived, the first tonic to come Thatcher's way since Dr. Mercado. Despite his ensemble, which he, his wife, or Pierre Cardin thought suitable for northern New England, he was not resentful about being called back to town. Far from it, he was grateful.

"Sure, they've got mountains," he said, with the Bronx boy's live-and-let-live acceptance of non-urban topography, "but they've got a lot of people from Boston, too. Okay, here I am. Give me whatever I haven't read."

Since Jackson was action oriented, Thatcher let Charlie fill him in on the taxi ride. He himself felt obliged to hold the fort, in case Howard Vandevanter needed more reinforcements. Before he could accustom himself to the unnatural silence at the Sloan, it was broken. Walter Bowman came padding in.

"What are you doing here?"

The simultaneous question flushed much information on both sides.

Walter tried, unconvincingly, to pretend that something new in the great Union Funding debacle required his holiday presence. By the time they got to the truth—Mrs. Bowman's brother, sister-in-law, and five nieces were visiting from Cedar Rapids—and lightly touched on Howard Vandevanter's plight, Charlie Trinkam was back.

"That was fast," Walter commented.

"Even when he's wearing baby blue pants, Paul doesn't fool around," Charlie replied. "He had Vandevanter out in six minutes."

"Not bad for a Columbus Day morning," said Walter. "Where are they now?"

"As I understand it," said Charlie, pretending to be more innocent than the Sloan would have tolerated, "Paul wanted to talk to Vandevanter about a few things. They were heading for Paul's office."

"Well," said Walter, "that settles whether Paul has been hired. Don't look at me like that, Charlie. You know how Paul strikes some people—especially when he's wearing everything color-coded to match his eyes."

"Vandevanter looked as if he was in pretty bad shape," said Charlie seriously.

"Jail," Walter commented sadly, "is always something

that happens to other guys." Possibly he was thinking of Union Funding, possibly of more historic institutions.

"He said," Charlie reported, "that once he finished up with Paul, he wanted to get back to Dreyer."

"Very reasonable," said Thatcher, without asking about movements from one jurisdiction to another. He could trust Paul Jackson to have that taped.

"I've brought you the papers, in case you didn't get them." Charlie tossed them on the desk.

Even the prolix *New York Times* could not add much to the terse statement by the police department. Their redoubtable files, however, had yielded too much information about Amory Shaw and Dick Frohlich. The headline was suitably sober, but in many ways more deadly than the *Post:* DREYER TROUBLES GROW.

21

Miss Corsa had long since proved herself immune to the frailty that makes so many Monday mornings a penance. Even the Tuesday after a long weekend was child's play for her.

"Did you have a pleasant holiday?" Thatcher inquired when he arrived at the Sloan.

Despite a noticeably sunburned nose, Miss Corsa had put frivolity behind her. A bank, in her opinion, was no place to describe family barbecues. Instead, she set about making up for lost time.

"You have a letter on your desk from Ziprodt and Ziprodt," she reported. "They also called just before you came in, Mr. Thatcher, to ask when you'll be able to make a pretrial deposition."

Thanks to his recent exertions, mention of any law firm sent Thatcher's thoughts scudding in one direction.

"Pretrial deposition?" he exclaimed, halting on the threshold of his own office. "Vandevanter wasn't even charged."

Like the rest of the world, Miss Corsa had read all about Howard Vandevanter. But the plight of the Dreyer Chocolate Company and its president was interesting to her only because of its inextricable linkage, through the Leonard Dreyer Trust, to Mr. Thatcher. Accordingly, she might have been accusing him of nameless crimes as she replied:

"This is *not* about Mr. Vandevanter. It's a suit by a Mr. Gary Hunneman against the Checker Cab Company, and Avis."

Observing that this did not jog his memory, she helpfully added: "Mr. Sims wants you to return his call about the accident."

That, of course, did it. Thatcher recalled the consultation with Bartlett Sims, about the Leonard Dreyer Trust, that had culminated in leaking antifreeze and an unpaid cabby. Mr. Gary Hunneman, presumably, was the one who had been exercising his God-given right to drive a rented car in the heart of Manhattan. Not content with precipitating a rear-end collision, he was now proposing to make legal history.

Thatcher resolved to let the Sloan's law department deal with this triumph of egocentricity and, if possible, to avoid Bartlett Sims. But he was not destined to rival Miss Corsa's assiduous attention to duty. Before he could get to the material about furniture stripping franchises on his desk, another potential lawsuit rose up to smite him.

Fred Nagle's wrath made him impossible to decipher when Miss Corsa put him through. Fortunately, Helen Nagle was used to serving as simultaneous interpreter.

"I nagged Fred into calling you, John," she said frankly.

Thatcher replied that he was always happy to hear

from the Nagles. This was still true, despite disjointed cries of ferocity from the other extension.

"Just wait a minute, Fred," Helen said. "Let me explain it to John—"

"After forty-five years!"

"—so he can talk some sense to you. John, Fred wants to sue Dreyer."

Thatcher did not vent the first thought that surfaced—namely, that there seemed to be an epidemic of litigiousness abroad. Deliberately he said, "Don't I recall you telling me that Dreyer was a good outfit to deal with? I know Arrow Jobbers has been doing business with them for a long time—"

"Forty-five years!" Nagle choked.

Extracting a coherent account was not easy. Nevertheless, with valuable assistance from Helen, Thatcher finally got the picture. A routine invoice error, uncovered by Fred over the weekend, had sent him to Dreyer's billing department. To his amazement, Dreyer's billing department flatly refused Arrow Jobbers either refund or credit.

"Those dumb slobs!" Fred sputtered. "We're their biggest customer, except for the U.S. Army! What kind of way is this to treat me—"

"Maybe Dreyer is simply running out of money."

Thatcher's comment was intended to lighten the atmosphere. But, as Charlie Trinkam sauntered into the office, he saw that levity was misplaced. Charlie's eyebrows rose to new heights. Fred took it seriously, too.....

"Then let Dreyer declare bankruptcy!" he raged. "Until they do, if they think they're going to pull this sort of thing—over a lousy eight hundred bucks—they've got another think coming."

"Oh, for heaven's sake," Helen broke in. "Don't encourage him, John! We all know this is just one of those mistakes. And it will get settled. There's no use getting so excited! As for suing—"

Thatcher was anxious to second her efforts and redeem himself.

"You're right, Helen. I wouldn't be premature, Fred. You know how these computerized systems botch credits and refunds. Why, Miss Corsa was busy for days coping with Abercrombie & Fitch about their double charge on a tennis racket I bought . . ."

Fred Nagle, still seeing red, obviously itched to tell him what he could do with Abercrombie & Fitch, let alone his tennis racket. Hastily, Helen cut him off:

"Absolutely. And, John, you do agree that Fred should wait for at least a few days, don't you?"

"I'm calling my lawyer—"

"What about a cooling-off period?" Thatcher inserted. If Ziprodt & Ziprodt were any example, Fred's lawyers would be drawing up attachment papers before lunch. "Say, until the end of this week."

This was too eminently reasonable for Fred to dismiss out of hand, much as he would have liked to. When Helen finally led him away, he had grudgingly agreed to four days' grace.

"That's true enough," Charlie ruminated. "About how credits and refunds foul things up. But the billing department must be breaking down at Dreyer. Everything else seems to be."

As if on signal, Miss Corsa rang through. "Governor Yeoman is on the line," she reported. "I've told him that you're in conference . . ."

This was not a graceful bow to Charlie's place in the great Sloan hierarchy but Miss Corsa's concession that, in some instances, Thatcher could decide for himself which calls to accept.

"Put him through, please," he directed, while Charlie shamelessly prepared to eavesdrop.

Yeoman came on abrasively. "Do you know where Vandevanter is!"

Thatcher hoped it was not Brazil.

"He's in his office at Dreyer—that's where he is!" Yeoman said, inviting Thatcher to share his outrage.

"What did you expect?" Thatcher rejoined. "He got out on the material witness charge—and the police weren't

169

willing to charge him with murder. I assume Vandevanter had a satisfactory explanation for that meeting with Amory Shaw—"

"You may assume that, but I don't!" Yeoman snapped. "He certainly hasn't taken me into his confidence!"

He was trespassing beyond the limits of Thatcher's patience. "That's understandable, isn't it?"

There was a pause, then Yeoman modulated his voice and his position.

"This is a very serious situation here at Dreyer. Of course, if Howard had remained in jail, we would have done everything we could for him."

Charlie, who could hear every word, chortled aloud. If Yeoman's weekend performance constituted wholehearted support, Vandevanter was well advised to keep his own counsel.

"Nevertheless," Yeoman pressed on, undeterred by the lack of response, "with Vandevanter in jail, there was a de facto vacancy in the office of president . . ."

He let this dangle enticingly, so Thatcher obliged with an unfriendly: "Go on."

At last, he was getting through. Yeoman was growing defensive: "I've been in touch with several Dreyer directors. Most of us agree that the board is going to have to take steps."

"What do you propose?" Thatcher was fair-minded enough to recognize some merit in Yeoman's position. No corporation wants its letters to stockholders signed by a man out on bail.

"Howard has to take a leave of absence!" Yeoman was emphatic. "Unless he prefers to resign outright!"

Thatcher scented a plot to force Vandevanter out for good. "How long a leave of absence do you have in mind?"

But even while he asked, he knew what the answer had to be. "Until all taint of suspicion is removed," Yeoman retorted instantly. "It's the least Dreyer has a right to demand."

"And what if the police never solve Amory Shaw's murder?"

Yeoman pointedly let the question stand. Then: "I'm still trying to get in touch with the other directors. I'll be in contact with you later, John."

"A trial balloon," commented Thatcher after he had gotten rid of Yeoman. "Yeoman was delighted to see Vandevanter in jail. I'm beginning to wonder if he doesn't want to see him hanged."

"You know," mused Charlie, "I've always thought Vandevanter was a pretty cold fish. But if he didn't kill Amory Shaw, well—you've got to feel sorry for the guy. He's got Leo Gilligan making noises like Amory Shaw. And Yeoman is doing his damnedest to shaft him. Now Fred Nagle is gunning for him, too. On top of all that, he's got nature boy taking pictures of him with Amory Shaw—just ten minutes before the murder."

Before Thatcher could comment, Miss Corsa again had a bulletin from the outer world. This time it was the Avis car rental company. They too wanted Mr. Thatcher's testimony in connection with a lawsuit they were mounting against the Checker Cab Company.

"Refer them to the Law Department," said Thatcher, automatically.

Both Miss Corsa and Charlie knew him well enough to be suspicious of his abstracted tone. Miss Corsa, after one look, departed to revise the day's schedule. Charlie, however, drew nearer.

"What's made you stiffen like a bird dog, John?"

There were many ways for Thatcher to answer this.

Bartlett Sims, and one minor traffic mishap . . .

Fred Nagle, and a botched shipment of Old Glory . . .

Or even Charlie Trinkam, and a connoisseur's account of strange doings at the Cocoa Exchange . . .

Instead, Thatcher said: "You and Yeoman both reminded me that I've never seen this damning photograph by Phibbs."

"And you want to," Charlie supplied, rising to accompany him. "Don't tell me why—let me guess."

22

Few people find visits to police headquarters so rewarding.

"Well," Charlie commented an hour later. "You can see why they arrested Vandevanter. Phibbs may not be any Karsh of Ottawa, but that's one helluva picture."

John Thatcher, still studying it, had to agree. Craig Phibbs had his deficiencies as a social commentator. He was a master of the camera.

"It's a shame to waste skill like this on that pretentious juvenilia of his," Thatcher murmured. "There aren't many photographers technically equipped to catch anything with such fatal accuracy."

Phibbs' pinpoint focus had etched in every detail. Yet, at the same time, his total field projected its own balance and tension. Amory Shaw was just exiting from an office. He was half-turned, so that a forbidding frown showed almost full face. Howard Vandevanter, on the other hand, could be recognized only by his distinctive yellow hair, and the barest suggestion of his profile. These two figures, in the forefront of the photograph, were the critical mass, but Shaw's arm was stretched back, his hand still resting on the doorknob. The viewer's eye was led hypnotically to the door, the office number—then to the wall clock overhead, with its hands recording minute and hour for all time. This was a portrait of Amory Shaw minutes before he stumbled onto the floor of the Cocoa Exchange with a knife in his back.

"You were right, John. If that doesn't spotlight a murderer, I don't know what does," Charlie observed.

"The police certainly thought so," said Thatcher dryly. "Let's see if they're willing to look at this picture from another point of view."

Detective Dennis Udall's good offices had given Thatcher and Charlie access to Craig Phibbs' handiwork. Thatcher had solid grounds for thinking that Udall would listen to his hypothesis with courtesy. But what would be accomplished by such an audience? Thatcher's argument rested heavily on his own intuition about probabilities— particularly, probabilities concerning dollars and cents. Detective Udall, understandably, would want hard proof. And that proof, if it existed, was unavailable. It lay buried in the offices of firms too important to let outsiders riffle through files in search of criminal evidence.

He caught Charlie off base by coming to a sudden halt. "I have a better idea," he said, wheeling and heading for the exit.

When Charlie caught up with him, demanding an explanation, Thatcher replied: "Stop to think. True, there is plenty of evidence here in New York. But it will take court orders to dig it up. What we need now is evidence out in plain sight."

Charlie protested. "John, you're not planning an end play around the police, are you?"

"I am simply going to speed things up by a perfectly legitimate short cut," Thatcher declared.

"How legitimate?" Charlie asked dubiously.

His skepticism was mirrored by Miss Corsa when she obeyed Thatcher's instructions and placed a long-distance call—to Dreyer, New York.

It is one thing to set machinery in motion. It is another to sit around, waiting for results. Happily, Thatcher and Charlie were spared this endurance test.

Charlie came rushing back to Thatcher's office brandishing the note he had found on his desk.

"Leo Gilligan," he said tersely. "He wants me to come down to the Cocoa Exchange as soon as I can."

For one startled moment, Thatcher frowned at him.

173

Then common sense reasserted itself. "It has to be coincidence," he concluded. "It's far too early . . ."

Superstitiously, both men checked their watches. Scarcely an hour and a half had passed since Thatcher's initial call to Dreyer.

"Maybe yes, maybe no," said Charlie mysteriously. "Light a fire and you don't know how fast it's going to spread. Anyway I thought you might like to come along with me."

Thatcher did want to accompany him.

"Although," he said, after informing Miss Corsa that he would be out for the rest of the day, "I don't really know what I expect to find."

Whatever it was, it was not Governor Curtis Yeoman.

Yet his was undeniably the voice thundering from the late Amory Shaw's office when Charlie and Thatcher arrived.

"I wonder—" Charlie began.

But Thatcher simply straight-armed the door. It was too late for wondering, now.

"Yeoman, you want to play games in Dreyer—it's okay with me! But don't try dragging me into your dirty work—"

"Gilligan, I'm telling you—"

"You're not telling me anything!"

Leo Gilligan, unlike Amory Shaw, was not the man for retreats to private offices and hushed consultations. This shouting match with Curtis Yeoman was being played out before Gene Orcutt, Russ Martini, and an enthralled Mrs. Macomber.

Yeoman was already restive at this gallery. When it was enlarged, he swung angrily away from Gilligan to glower at Thatcher and Charlie.

"What are you doing here?" he demanded aggressively.

"That's precisely what I was going to ask you," Thatcher retorted icily.

"I'll tell you what he's doing," said Gilligan rudely.

"He's trying to take over Dreyer—that's what he's doing."

Yeoman sucked in his breath. But he was incapable of matching Gilligan's disregard for witnesses. With a nervous glance toward Martini and Orcutt, he struggled to reintroduce normality by addressing Thatcher.

"As I told you earlier, Thatcher, we're in the middle of a crisis. I decided that the wisest thing to do was come down here and talk things over with Gilligan—"

A contemptuous grunt from Gilligan deflected him.

"After all, it takes no time at all to get here from Dreyer . . ."

"No," said Thatcher evenly, "it doesn't, does it?"

Yeoman pressed on: "So I flew down here to consult with Gilligan."

But he was getting no support from that quarter.

"As far as I'm concerned, Howard Vandevanter is the president of Dreyer, and he stays that way until the board tells me otherwise!"

"We will, of course, be convening the board . . ."

"Talk to me then!"

Curtis Yeoman was chafing at the onlookers; he was angered by Gilligan's unexpected resistance. But, above all, he was single-minded.

"What about the interim! You mean that you're going to take orders from Vandevanter—"

Gilligan's head went back. "I'm not taking orders from anyone!"

"You may be doing millions of dollars of trading in the next few days," Yeoman expostulated.

Before the combat could resume, there was intervention from the sidelines.

"Look," said Russ Martini with an uncomfortable smile, "don't get me wrong. But this is none of my business. If you're going to have a takeover at Dreyer, that's up to you. But I think maybe I'll just push off."

"Hell, no!" Gilligan objected immediately. "I want to go over the day's sales. That's what Dreyer pays me for—not a lot of infighting. Orcutt, have you totaled up the March contracts? And Shirley, get me the folder on our cash position . . ."

His whirlpool of activity shunted Yeoman aside.

"Doesn't he ever work in his own office?" Yeoman complained as Mrs. Macomber nudged him aside to pull out a drawer.

Thatcher did not bother to reply. Instead, he checked his watch again. By now, he was fairly sure, he was somewhere in a countdown. But where, only time would tell. Charlie, however, was still intent on spadework.

"Tell me, Governor," he said chattily, "does Howard Vandevanter know about these little efforts of yours?"

With a dangerous glitter in his eye, Yeoman answered: "I have made representations to Howard about stepping aside for the duration. When he categorically refused, I felt free to make every effort to have him replaced."

But, Thatcher decided, there was a furtive character to Yeoman's attempted coup that was dissonant with this self-righteous pronouncement.

If Thatcher's telephone call had borne fruit, the point would be moot.

"Well, that wraps up the essentials," Russ Martini said, straightening from the notes spread on Mrs. Macomber's desk. "I know you want to check out the open interest, but that can wait until tomorrow."

"We'll go over it right now," Gilligan ordered. "You heard me tell Governor Yeoman we've got work to do. You sit down and I'll send out for coffee . . ."

Gilligan could not resist this unnecessary slap at Yeoman, even when it entailed a glancing blow at Charlie and Thatcher, too.

Charlie was not playing along. "Are you offering John and me coffee, too, Leo? Don't forget, you invited us."

Gilligan's call to the Sloan had argued only prudent wariness in his dealings with the Dreyer Chocolate Company. But now he seemed taut with pressure.

Before he could reply, Gene Orcutt blurted anxiously: "Do you want me to go out for coffee, Mr. Gilligan?"

This homely note should have relaxed Gilligan.

Strangely enough it did not. "Sure, sure!" he said. "But, Russ, I want you to stick around."

Whether he was conscious of it or not, Orcutt was rattled by the passions furiously crisscrossing the room. He was bending down to retrieve the pencil he had dropped when Yeoman snapped:

"What's that!"

Everybody turned to stare at him.

"I heard something, I tell you."

Mrs. Macomber looked puzzled. "That noise?" she asked. "That's just the elevator stopping."

"Are you expecting someone, Yeoman?" Gilligan demanded nastily.

Yeoman shook his head. But as the footsteps approached, anticipation gripped the entire room.

The opening door should have punctured the tension. But even Thatcher, who knew what to expect, was taken aback.

In the small office, it seemed as if Howard Vandevanter had brought an army with him. There were men in uniform on all sides.

Gilligan took one step forward and froze in his tracks. Russ Martini was rooted where he stood. Gene Orcutt pressed himself against the wall.

Only Vandevanter was perfectly natural. Ignoring his companions, and the rest of the room's occupants, he bore down on John Thatcher.

"Now, look here, Thatcher. I've done just what you asked. But I'll be damned if I go any further without getting some explanation."

Vandevanter's movement revealed the group previously obscured. A middle-aged woman stood between Captain Huggins from Dreyer and Detective Dennis Udall. She swept the room with one searching glance. Then:

"That's him!" she said unhesitatingly. "I'd stake my life on it!"

23

Russ Martini's voice was shrill and ugly. "I never saw this woman before in my life."

"Then what about the girl at the car rental agency?" challenged Captain Huggins. "She picked your picture from more than a dozen."

"I don't know what you're talking about."

"That line won't get you anywhere. There's the license number, too." Huggins was disappointed in his first killer. "You left a trail a mile wide."

Martini's lips folded into a tight, grim line. "Go to hell!"

"Just a minute, you two." Detective Udall had shouldered his way forward, pulling a card from his pocket. "Before you say anything else, Mr. Martini, I am about to advise you of your rights. You have the right to . . ."

When he finished intoning, Russ Martini slumped in his chair without uttering a word.

Curtis Yeoman could not resist any opportunity to sound authoritative. "You need a lawyer," he said. "Is there anyone you'd like us to call?"

It was enough to remind Howard Vandevanter of a grievance. "You're damned helpful about lawyers so long as it isn't me in jail," he said in tones that would have blistered paint.

Rarely had a charitable impulse been more untimely. And, thought Thatcher, it wasn't as if Curtis Yeoman had so many.

Happily Leo Gilligan rescued them all. "The one you want is Jim Mears, Martini's partner," he told the assembled authorities. "Why don't you stop in their office across the hall? That's okay with you, isn't it, Russ?"

This stratagem cleared the room of the police, the unknown woman, and Martini. It did not deflect Howard Vandevanter.

"Now I've been very patient, Thatcher. I've done everything you wanted without asking questions," he said untruthfully. "But what the hell is going on? What is all this about a car rental agency? Amory Shaw was killed right in this building."

"But Dick Frohlich wasn't," countered Thatcher.

Vandevanter blinked. He had been concentrating on the murder imperiling him.

Cautiously Yeoman ventured back into the conversation. "Do you mean to say that Russ Martini killed Frohlich? But he wasn't even in Dreyer with us."

"Which makes him all the more suspect. What do we know about Frohlich's murderer?" Thatcher prepared to enumerate. "We know that he called motels in Dreyer to find out where Dick Frohlich was registered. That immediately suggests he was not in the official party. In addition, the murderer spent a long time lurking in the underbrush waiting for Frohlich to come home. That was unnecessary if the murderer had a room in that courtyard—as you and I and Amory Shaw did."

There was a pause. Yeoman's unspoken question trembled on his lips, but he was not risking Howard Vandevanter's wrath again. With some amusement, Thatcher let him stew in his own juice for several moments before continuing.

"Vandevanter, here, could also have avoided the bushes. Quite apart from the fact that he could have dictated Frohlich's movements so that they met elsewhere, he would never have chosen a murder plan so peculiarly dangerous to him."

The president of Dreyer was seeing offense everywhere. "Why would it be more dangerous for me than for anyone else?" he asked resentfully.

Thatcher was beginning to think that the Leonard

Dreyer Trust asked more of its trustees than it was going to get.

"The motel was filled with Dreyer employees, every one of whom would recognize you," he replied crisply. "Furthermore, you would have had to pass under that floodlit archway twice. Most men could hurry by with their heads down. But you? Could you afford to have a witness say that the only thing he remembered was a man with a head of brilliant yellow hair?"

"Oh," Vandevanter still looked unaccountably affronted.

Gilligan took over the questioning. "All right. I can see you've made a case for the murderer not being officially in Dreyer. But that leaves almost the whole world."

"Certainly—until you move on to consider the motive. Dick Frohlich had just returned to the country after an extended absence. By the end of one working day, he was anxiously trying to communicate with Amory Shaw—and also telling people that something was wrong at Dreyer's New York office."

"Shaw was the one he'd go to if—"

"I assumed that meant that Frohlich—"

Vandevanter and Yeoman had collided in midspeech. Governor Curtis Yeoman yielded.

"It's not the kind of thing I like to say, now that he's dead," Vandevanter began circuitously, "but for a while I wondered if Frohlich had found some mess in Shaw's department, and was giving him a chance to clean it up. Naturally I didn't think that at first. But when Amory Shaw began to be so secretive about what was going on in New York, well, then I did begin to wonder." He sat back and glared at Yeoman.

"Now, Howard," said Yeoman, striving to regain his old air of command, "you've got to remember that Amory was used to being completely independent. What seemed like secrecy to you was only a natural defense of his prerogatives."

"No, I cannot agree that Shaw's behavior was natural." Thatcher had decided not to give Yeoman any more leeway. "Why should it have been, given the situation with which he was coping? When Frohlich complained about dirty work in New York, he could only have been referring to his own department, or Shaw's. And Frohlich's office turned out to be in apple-pie order. To the outside world, that meant skullduggery *by* Shaw or *to* Shaw. And he knew it. Amory Shaw was determined to scotch the scandal himself. As Yeoman says, he was jealous of his prerogatives. With a new president he was certainly not going to undermine his strength by having someone else conduct the exposure."

Vandevanter rose to a handsome gesture. "He was right to worry. I didn't like New York being so independent. If I'd found a loophole Shaw had overlooked, I would have used that to weaken his position with the board."

"And a loophole that resulted in murder would certainly have impressed the board with its gravity," Thatcher said grimly. "But Shaw was a very puzzled man. He could not put his finger on the corruption. That's why he went haring off to Frohlich's relatives, in hopes of finding a clue. And, in fact, he got one."

Yeoman's head came up alertly. "What was that?"

"The trade with Martini on the day before the murder."

"But Shaw himself told us that was just peanuts," Vandevanter protested.

"Yes. The trade itself meant nothing, only the timing. Unfortunately before Shaw could concentrate on that, he was diverted by news of the row with Orcutt. That turned his thoughts closer to home."

Everybody swiveled to look at Gene Orcutt, who tried becoming invisible by sheer willpower.

"Well, Gene," Leo Gilligan said easily, "now's the time to come clean. What did you and Dick Frohlich tangle about?"

"But that wasn't the problem," Orcutt blurted, then hurried to cover his lapse. "There wasn't any real tangle. I came back to the office to find Frohlich rooting around the orders for the day. Knowing how Mr. Shaw disliked anyone seeing them, I tried to take them away. And he blew up like a rocket."

Gilligan had not made a fortune in cocoa by ignoring lapses. "Then what was the problem?" he pressed remorselessly.

Orcutt looked for help. When none was forthcoming, he said stubbornly, "There wasn't any."

"Perhaps I can help," Thatcher intervened. "When Shaw was looking for a weakness in his office, his thoughts first turned to you. He knew that you traded on your own account?"

"Everybody does," Orcutt gritted.

"Yes, indeed. But I expect he could also make a good guess as to the results of your trading."

"What does that have to do with it?" Yeoman demanded.

Gilligan squinted down the length of his cigar. "Been losing your shirt?" he asked Orcutt gently. "Not meeting your margin calls?"

There was a painful pause.

"I don't know why you say that," Orcutt muttered at last.

"I've listened to some of your suggestions about the Dreyer account," Gilligan replied amiably.

Orcutt flushed. "Well, Mr. Shaw certainly never listened to my suggestions. But when I asked to put off my vacation, he seemed to guess why."

"Couldn't afford one, eh?" Gilligan nodded to himself. "That figures."

Vandevanter was staring at his hand-picked junior executive in horror. "Do you mean that's all you've been hiding? In the middle of a murder investigation, you've been acting mysteriously simply because of losing money?"

Gilligan was amused. "I think Gene figured that wouldn't be much of a recommendation for Shaw's successor."

"Shaw realized that Orcutt was the perfect paid informant," Thatcher explained. "But here he hit a stumbling block. The one thing everybody assured us was that Shaw never took Orcutt—or anyone else—into his confidence about his trading."

Orcutt at last found his tongue. "I didn't expect him to, before the trading. But at least he could have explained to me afterward."

"Wait until you're over sixty-five and they force a young assistant on you," Thatcher advised. "But there we have the whole situation as it looked to Shaw until the day he was murdered. It only took one departure from routine on that day to make the whole thing crystal clear to him."

"Now wait a minute." Leo Gilligan had retired into his own furious thoughts, traces of which could be seen in his furrowed brow and tapping finger.

Thatcher watched these efforts appreciatively.

"A departure . . . ? Oh! I get you. Shaw came on the floor before he was ready to buy in person. He must have caught Martini in the act."

"Exactly!" Thatcher beamed. "Now what do you think happened before the first murder? Remember the sequence of Frohlich's movements. First, he saw Shaw, then he did some trading of his own, through his broker, Russ Martini. The next thing, he's back across the hall, reviewing Shaw's trade for the day. Finally he urgently wants to consult Shaw."

The furrows and tappings were things of the past. Gilligan's brow was cloudless, his expression serene. "It's as plain as the nose on your face," he concluded.

"Possibly to you," said Curtis Yeoman huffily. "Would it be too much trouble to enlighten the rest of us? I think I speak for Howard as well as myself."

Appeals for solidarity to Howard were not going to be honored for some time. Vandevanter gave him one jaundiced look and dissociated himself.

"I think I see what you're driving at," he said, as irritatingly as possible. "Frohlich caught both ends of some transaction." Wisely, he decided to leave it at that.

"Sure," said Gilligan. He turned to Thatcher. "I assume you mean that Martini was using the information for his own profit."

"More than that. He was putting his own trades through first, regardless of the consequences to Dreyer. The worst thing a commodity broker can do."

"They're all bastards," Gilligan said largely. "But it makes plenty of sense. This is the way it worked out. Shaw phones an order to Martini in Frohlich's hearing. Martini doesn't know that. Then Frohlich hears Martini placing the Dreyer trade ten minutes too late. It doesn't click right away. When it does, he wants to check with Shaw's records. He still doesn't have a watertight case, but he's got plenty to talk to Shaw about. Thinking that they'll both be at the banquet, he leaves for Dreyer.

"In the midst of all this, Martini learns that Frohlich wants to speak with Shaw urgently. There were plenty of people—"

"Sir?"

Again every eye was on Orcutt. He gulped unhappily. "I think maybe I can explain that. I told Mr. Shaw that Frohlich was looking for him in front of Mr. Martini."

Gilligan glared at his subordinate. "And what else did you tell Martini?"

But this time Orcutt could shake his head decisively. "It wasn't me. It was Mr. Shaw," he declared confusingly. "He was in a bad mood. He kind of snapped at me not to interrupt. It couldn't be very important, he said, because Frohlich had been here only a little while ago, when the Russians and the Americans linked up in space. Then he sent me on some errand. I think he repeated Frohlich's joke as soon as he got me out of the way."

"There you have it," Thatcher said, pleased at this unexpected corroboration. "Every radio in New York was tuned to the docking. I'm sure Martini's office was no exception. To his horror, he realized that Frohlich had been privy to both ends of the transaction and had immediately set out in search of Shaw. That was quite enough for Russ Martini to know he was in deep trouble unless he could prevent the meeting. I assume that Shaw would have had no doubts about what to do."

"Good God, no!" Curtis Yeoman exploded. "Amory was a fanatic about the integrity of the Cocoa Exchange. He would have had Martini stripped of his license and probably sent to jail. Wayne Glasscock wouldn't have shilly-shallied with a complaint made by Amory Shaw."

Howard Vandevanter was more concerned with Dreyer than with Wayne Glasscock. "But this must have been going on for some time. How did Martini get away with it?"

"He was protected by Shaw's own habits of secrecy," Thatcher reminded him. "Besides, he must have been prudent enough to wait for a confused market when he could explain away—"

Thatcher halted as the door was flung open. Mrs. Macomber was too excited for apologies.

"Oh, Mr. Gilligan," she stammered. "Mr. Mears is on the line. He's all upset. Cocoa has just hit ninety! He can't leave the floor, and no one's in his office. What should he do about your stop orders? Is he still your broker? He doesn't know—"

"Christ!" Gilligan was surging from his chair, beating out a shower of sparks from his cigar. "Orcutt, I want you with me."

"Yes, sir!"

"It happened even sooner than I expected. Boy, is Dreyer going to make a pretty penny out of this!" Gilligan's running commentary was a song of triumph as he stalked toward the hall. "If we can catch it before ninety-one, we'll be in gravy."

"I'm coming with you," declared Howard Vandevanter, also on his feet. "It's high time I learned more about the Cocoa Exchange."

"Then just come and don't interfere," commanded Gilligan without breaking stride.

All three of them swept out of the office without a backward glance.

"But you haven't finished," Yeoman protested to

Thatcher. "What about the car? What about that woman?"

Thatcher and Charlie were already shrugging themselves into coats.

"I don't think anybody is interested just now," Thatcher said gently.

But it is well known that foreigners have more tenacity of purpose than flibbertigibbet Americans. In the crowded week following Russ Martini's arrest, John Thatcher did not forget Dr. Umberto Mercado and Signor Giorgio Alizio. The Leonard Dreyer Trust owed them a great deal, and two men who had yearned to see the Royal Dutch Motel must be going mad with the newspaper accounts they were reading in their hotel rooms. A telephone call confirmed this suspicion, eliciting a torrent of Italianate gratitude for an invitation to view the Cocoa Exchange.

"And it is all just as they said," marveled Alizio after a Cook's tour featuring Martini & Mears, Amory Shaw's office, and the perch from which Thatcher had seen a man die on the floor of the Exchange. "Your *Daily News* and *Times* and *New York Post* and *Wall Street Journal*."

Leo Gilligan, who had been acting as usher, stopped pouring Scotch. "If you've been following all those papers, you must know more about the murder than anyone else."

"Like hell we do!" Dr. Mercado's hands might not have been designed to fondle Etruscan vases, but they could make some quite expressive negative gestures. "We know why the murders were committed—"

"Well, that's simple enough," Gilligan interrupted. "Russ Martini had his hand in the till and was willing to kill anybody who caught him at it."

"We know how they were committed, we know who committed them, but," Mercado said accusingly to Thatcher, "we don't know how you broke the thing apart."

"And the car," Alizio insisted. "How did that enter?"

"The police chief in Dreyer was on to that point, right away," Thatcher replied. "If one man killed Frohlich and drove away from Dreyer in a car, how did he get back? And if he didn't have to come back, then he had never officially been in Dreyer. When I became suspicious of Martini, I remembered Charlie Trinkam had overheard a fuss in Martini's office about the bill for a rental car."

"Always there are fusses about rental cars," Alizio said resignedly. "Never do they charge the correct amount, always too much or too little."

"Very true. But Martini had received a personal refund that he did not wish to explain to his secretary. You can understand why he was bothered. He had deliberately not used his company credit card to prevent any flowback to his office. He did not want his secretary asking why he was driving a rented car around upstate New York on the night of Frohlich's murder. He had paid in cash, and then the wretched refund rose to haunt him."

Mercado was still troubled. "I can see how it was a pain in the neck for him. But how did it help you?"

"I remembered Captain Huggins' interest in the murder car. So, with the help of Howard Vandevanter, I asked him a question. If he had the identity of the murderer and the name of the rental agency, could he gather any proof? His answer was enthusiastic. He was already assuming the murderer had checked into some motel at a discreet distance from Dreyer. With Russ Martini's picture, he located that woman in under an hour—she, of course, was the motel owner. Then, with the license number, he back-tracked Martini to the Hertz agency in Utica. Remember, Martini had decided to follow Frohlich to Dreyer on the spur of the moment. He had no time for elaborate planning. He flew out to Utica in the commuting rush, hired a car and committed his murder. The next morning he was up early enough to check in the car and return on another commuter flight. Apparently he was away from home at night often enough so that raised no problems."

"Very enlightening," said Alizio, as polite as ever.

"No, it isn't," said Dr. Mercado more candidly. "How did you get suspicious of Martini in the first place?"

"By noticing a pattern in the Cocoa Exchange that pointed straight to him."

"Now, wait just one minute," growled Leo Gilligan. "No offense intended, Thatcher, but if you noticed a pattern in cocoa last week, Amory Shaw should have spotted it within an hour."

"I had one great advantage over Shaw," Thatcher pointed out. "In order to see the pattern, you needed two murders. The cocoa market was going the same way on each occasion."

"The boys were waiting for Shaw to come in and buy," Gilligan agreed. "Of course, it was more dramatic the second time. Everybody was hoping for split-second news about Shaw's timing."

"And who necessarily had it—on each occasion?"

"Russ Martini." Gilligan sounded like a judge passing sentence.

"But there was another piece to the pattern. We had ample evidence that Dick Frohlich emerged from Russ Martini's office and shortly thereafter had a fight with Gene Orcutt. In Orcutt's words, he was ready to go off like a rocket. Then we heard that Shaw, immediately before his death, had a fight with Howard Vandevanter. I found myself wondering where *he* had just come from. And the picture in the possession of the police told me."

Gilligan had a vivid recollection of the incarceration of Dreyer's president. "But I thought the important thing about that picture was that it showed the two of them scrapping just before the murder."

"That was Phibbs' interpretation. He himself is not a very perceptive observer, but his camera is faultless. The picture did not show Vandevanter's face at all. What it did show was Amory Shaw in a towering rage, emerging from Martini's office. In other words, both murder victims had received bad news somehow connected with Martini shortly before they were killed. Actually, Shaw had discovered Martini's double-dealing on the floor. As soon as he could, he went in search of Martini to have it out with him. He did not find Martini in his office. Unfortunately he did find him a few minutes later, in an empty corridor."

"A tough break," said Mercado with ready sympathy. "If he'd cornered him in front of a lot of witnesses, there would have been a different ending for both of them."

Leo Gilligan was not prepared to let the conversation become melancholy. "When you consider that Phibbs put the finger on Vandevanter, and Yeoman compounded the job by trying to pretend the front office squabble was still going on, you have to hand it to Howard."

His tone was ironic enough to make Thatcher suspicious. "How is that?"

"Haven't you heard?" asked Gilligan, all innocence. "Seems that Phibbs wanted some cooperation for a documentary he's doing. And Vandevanter gave him Yeoman."

It was Thatcher's turn to be nonplussed. "Do you mean to say that Yeoman agreed?"

"Vandevanter fed him a line about cultural activity for educational TV, but it was Phibbs who sold him."

"How?" asked Thatcher and Mercado in unison, unwilling to believe that Phibbs could sell candles in a power blackout.

"He said he had to have Yeoman's eyebrows." Gilligan twinkled benignly at his incredulous audience. "I think Curtis just couldn't resist."

How to do <u>almost</u> everything

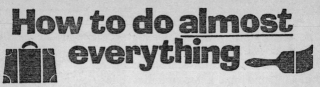

What are the latest time and money-saving shortcuts for painting, papering, and varnishing floors, walls, ceilings, furniture? (See pages 102-111 of HOW TO DO *Almost* EVERYTHING.) What are the mini-recipes and the new ways to make food—from appetizers through desserts—exciting and delicious? (See pages 165-283.) How-to-do-it ideas like these have made Bert Bacharach, father of the celebrated composer (Burt), one of the most popular columnists in America.

 This remarkable new book, HOW TO DO *Almost* EVERYTHING, is a fact-filled collection of Bert Bacharach's practical aids, containing thousands of tips and hints— for keeping house, gardening, cooking, driving, working, traveling, caring for children. It will answer hundreds of your questions, briefly and lucidly.

How to do <u>almost</u> everything

Is chock-full of useful information—information on almost everything you can think of, arranged by subject in short, easy-to-read tidbits, with an alphabetical index to help you find your way around —and written with the famed Bacharach touch.

SEND FOR YOUR FREE EXAMINATION COPY TODAY

We invite you to mail the coupon below. A copy of HOW TO DO *Almost* EVERYTHING will be sent to you at once. If at the end of ten days you do not feel that this book is one you will treasure, you may return it and owe nothing. Otherwise, we will bill you $7.95, plus postage and handling. At all bookstores, or write to Simon and Schuster, Dept. S-52, 630 Fifth Ave., New York, N.Y. 10020.

SIMON AND SCHUSTER, Dept. S-52
630 Fifth Ave., New York, N.Y. 10020

Please send me a copy of HOW TO DO *ALMOST* EVERYTHING. If after examining it for 10 days, I am not completely delighted, I may return the book and owe nothing. Otherwise, you will bill me for $7.95 plus mailing costs.

Name...

Address.......................................

City...................State........Zip........

☐ *SAVE!* Enclose $7.95 now and we pay postage. Same 10-day privilege with full refund guaranteed. (N. Y. residents please add applicable sales tax.)

P 66/2

Your Inner Child of the Past

🏵 **Once you were a child.**

🏵 **That child still lives within you—influencing and interfering in your adult life.**

🏵 **This book tells you HOW TO SOLVE YOUR ADULT EMOTIONAL PROBLEMS by recognizing, accepting and managing the feelings of YOUR INNER CHILD OF THE PAST.**

BY W. HUGH MISSILDINE, M.D.

AMONG THE NEW IDEAS AND FRESH APPROACHES IN THIS BOOK ARE:

- There are four people in every marriage bed
- Every "lone wolf" has an unwelcome companion
- There are times when it's all wrong to try to "do better"
- How the "command-resistance" cycle of childhood leads to adult sexual frustration
- How to be the right kind of parent to your "inner child of the past"
- Six rules for happy family life

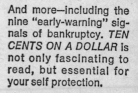
S 94/3